SWIFT

By Darrell Shaffer Jr.

DARRELL SHAFFER JR

ISBN 13: 9798646493171

I've come to understand a long time ago that the rules in this world aren't laid down like cold hard steel, like prison bars. The rules, you see they bend, they blur, but worst of all they often break.

- Isaiah "The King" Reed

CONTENTS

Chapter One   6

Chapter Two   13

Chapter Three   18

Chapter Four   23

Chapter Five   28

Chapter Six   33

Chapter Seven   40

Chapter Eight   45

Chapter Nine   49

Chapter Ten   56

Chapter Eleven   61

Chapter Twelve   65

Chapter Thirteen   70

Chapter Fourteen   75

Chapter Fifteen   77

Chapter Sixteen   82

Chapter Seventeen   85

Chapter Eighteen   89

Chapter Nineteen	94
Chapter Twenty	100
Chapter Twenty-One	105
Chapter Twenty-Two	110
Chapter Twenty-Three	114
Chapter Twenty-Four	121
About the Author	126

CHAPTER 1

"Bitch, you're are a fucking liar. You never ever ever got no pussy from Angilique. I never heard of you getting no pussy at all," Tevin yells at the whole block even if he's only speaking to Nate.

"Alright y'all chill out, I got a phone call," they finally take a break from a conversation that has gone on way too long. "It's Javon."

"What the spot looking like today," my uncle asks as if he's some kind of big shot.

"Not a mouse stirring. Meaning empty, like always."

"Watch your mouth boy, your numbers have been lacking. You're on thin ice as it is," he hangs up not wanting to hear what I have to say.

"Your Uncle Daddy," Tevin says, prompting Nate to laugh taking the pressure off him.

"Fuck him, and fuck you for even bringing that up. He put us out here as a joke. He just wants to make us look like fools."

"Well, he is your uncle and he is married to your mom now. So, uncle daddy," Nate adds and they both go back to laughing.

"But you're right, we need to be pushing on a different

corner. One that ain't so dead," Tevin says quickly changing the topic.

"This is 2019 not 1990. Crack is not selling like that anymore. Does he think this is Power? Who is getting rich selling crack right now? Nobody. Crack really is whack, for the smoker and the dealer. We knew that thirty years ago," I take a seat on the staircase next to them.

"We really should be selling something else, if we're going to be selling anything at all. Even if you could get rich selling crack, it wouldn't be us. We're just street level. We make enough to pay our bills," Nate was always the smart one.

"Basically, we either keep standing here and failing or we expand home to succeed," I have to verbally sum up his thoughts for myself sometimes.

"Look, didn't your pops get killed because he was trying to expand. He was a real stand up nigga, but don't follow in his footsteps on this one. It'll get you a spot right next his," Tevin adds.

"My pops didn't die because he was trying to expand. He died, because my uncle ain't shit. You know the whole thing has been funny from the moment we found out he was killed. Why would my pops be out in the country? He never fucked with the forest folk like that," I lean into my comments to make sure Tevin gets my point.

"Y'all should chill out or just fight one day. Y'all been butting heads since middle school and still hang out. Why? It doesn't make sense if you don't like each other" Nate asks in confusion.

"Because we're both friends you, dumbass," Tevin says rolling his eyes.

Nate blushes like that was the best compliment he's ever received. We drop the subject and go back to just talking about anything. Which girls were bad in high school, but aren't now. Who really came up in the world. What we would do if we weren't stuck here selling crack. Nate wants to own a night club for some reason. I know

Power is his favorite show, but this is getting ridiculous now. Tevin thinks he had a chance to go to the NBA. He's my friend, I let him believe it and I back him up. He never had a snowball's chance in hell to make it to the NBA. His jumper is trash, he can't dribble, no hops and he couldn't hit a free throw to save his life.

As for me, I don't know where I would have been. I wouldn't even be selling crack if my dad hadn't died. Tevin was already doing it on the side. Nate just followed me when I didn't have any other choices left. He was close to graduating from community college. I think he might have, I can't remember. At first, I only started selling because my uncle said that would be the only way I made money in his house. Pops never wanted me on the corners. He sent me off to college to be an accountant. Said he would need a money man he could trust and I could work in a big fancy office when I wasn't working for him. I just couldn't see myself being an account after he died. I dropped out and came home. Maybe I should have studied something else, been a lawyer or something.

Our favorite fiend Kevin makes his way up to us. He's our favorite, because we went to school with him. At the end of the day, he's still a good dude in his heart, just a shell of the man he could have been. He was already hooked on the stuff before any of us were thinking of selling. His cousins got him on the stuff back when he was like fourteen. That's fucked up. I don't know how you could do that to your own family. The fact that he's the same age as me, makes it harder to see. He could be doing so much more. I know I could too, but I'm not strung out on crack in 2019. Now he gets it from us, because he knows we're not going to give him anything that's been stepped on.

"I need a rock," he says.

"You got money," Tevin steps down to meet him.

"I got five on me. I can bring you the rest late," Kevin looks like he's up to something.

"You know the rules. It's $20 a rock."

"That shit ain't fair, you know me. How long you know me? 8 years? I ain't ever lied to you Big T," Kevin stomps his feet and turns his neck like he just made a point. He stands there with one hand out, and another on his waist. Waiting for Tevin to hand him a rock.

"Get the fuck out of here Kevin," Tevin says trying not laugh along with Nate and I.

"Or what? This is a free country. You should be glad to see me."

"Why would I be glad to see you," Tevin asks biting the inside of his cheek.

"Because, ain't nobody else buying crack from you. So, take these five dollars I earned, and bring me my rock."

"You know the price is twenty," Tevin says balling up his fist.

"These prices are ridiculous. If anyone else was still selling crack. I would no longer frequent this establishment," Kevin says turning his nose up as if he's trying to buy a Mercedes and not crack on a street corner.

"I ain't taking, five dollars, what else you got," Tevin asks.

"Nothing."

"Nothing?"

"Nothing, and I ain't sucking dick again."

"You ain't ever put your lips on my dick," Tevin push Kevin.

"Alright, here you go damn," Nate jumps up and takes the five dollars before passing Kevin a rock.

Everyone seems heated but I'm laughing. The whole thing is like a scene out of a movie or something. Kevin takes his rock and goes about his day while Nate tries to calm down Tevin. Almost like it was on cue, a black Mercedes with tinted windows stops across the street. In a neighborhood like this, it stands out like a sore thumb. Just hoping to be seen. I know the car, it belongs to Stack. My uncle's right-hand man and pain in my ass. Nate and Tevin take their seats on the steps knowing he's here to see me. I don't budge. I look at the car and wait for him to say he needs to see me. I'm not going to just run over there like some kind of puppy. That's what my uncle wants.

He rolls the window down and signals for me to come over with his finger. I'm not a dog so I just nod my head at him and look away. I'm not really interested in anything going on down the road, but I don't enjoy how Stack and my uncle see me as some kind of pet or charity case. I'm a grown man. They're going to learn that sooner or later.

"Javon, you see me over here," he yells with his big bald head hanging out the window. Looking like a pissed off milk dud.

"What you want," I make my way over to the car.

"Your numbers been low over here," he says bringing his yell down to a conversation level.

"Well, there's only twelve crackheads left in the city and they all live on the westside. 7 of them already got their rocks because they cook them at home. What do you expect?"

"I expect you to find a new way to move product."

"Police don't even look for crack dealers anymore. This stuff is done. We look stupid trying to hold on to the 90s."

"Just sell the shit," Stack sits back in his seat. He knows I'm right.

"To who man? Do you see anyone out here smoking? We're in the middle of gentrification. Hipsters don't want crack, they want pills and weed. Why are we still selling this?"

"Look, that's just the way Grady wants it done. It ain't the way your pops would have done it. It ain't the way I would do it. If your pops were here, or I was in charge you wouldn't even be allowed near a corner. But your dad is resting in peace, and I'm not in control. This is the way it is. We just have to deal with it," I don't know how Stack ended up selling drugs.

"Alright, I'll try to figure something out. Not for my

uncle, but for you Stack."

"I know you will, you're smart. If you want my advice, quit this shit. It's a dead-end street. I'm too far in to turn away. You can still go back to college, and take the two stooges with you. Think about it," Stack should have been a preacher or something. Always trying to share some kind of knowledge with people.

"I'll think about it," I can't promise I will.

"Good, now stop leaning on my car. I just had it washed and you're leaving hand prints."

Stack is an asshole, at least he's good at pretending to be one. In reality, he's a nice guy. Married his high school girlfriend, and had four kids. Never stepped out on her with a side chick, never put a hand on her or the kids. Tough guy for real, but always had the best birthday parties for his kids. Sent them off to college, didn't want them in this at all. Said if he ever goes down, his family won't go with him. If he had took over after my dad's death, I would have been able to sleep at night.

"What did he want," Tevin asks looking scared.

"Make more money, with your scary ass," I say with a laugh.

"Y'all wanna go get a pizza or something," Nate suggests. "Ain't nobody buying nothing else for the rest of the day."

"I can get a pizza," Tevin adds.

"Y'all go ahead, I'll catch up with y'all later," I don't really need to be around them arguing for another three hours. Pepperoni or sausage, deep dish or I'll agree with Nate because we like the same kind of pizza. Tevin will be mad and get a sperate pizza. I know how it'll go.

"Then let's go play video games. I got the new 2K," Tevin says.

"That sounds fun. Let's go," Nate cosigns.

"I'll pass."

"Look man, we're young. I'm good looking. Nate is smart. Javon you ain't got much but you're okay," Tevin starts with the jokes again

"Right, we got the whole world in front of us, and you're with us so you got the world in front of you too," Nate adds with a smile.

"Alright Timone and Pumba, we'll get pizza and play 2K. Y'all both trash anyway."

□

CHAPTER 2

I must have hit snooze too many times. I'm about an hour behind schedule. I should just cancel the whole thing really. I'd rather just sleep in. Sundays are supposed to be for resting right? I pully my phone off the charged and check my notifications. Mom has been blowing me up. Calls, voicemails and texts. She'll be okay. I roll out of bed and drop to the floor. I do a few pushups to get my blood flowing and wake myself up. A few situps and I'm good to go.

I make my way over to the closet and try to find something suitable to wear. Most of my clothes are just jeans and basic shirts. That's the stuff I wear, just because it's comfortable. It helps that it also keeps me from drawing attention, but a fresh cotton shirt on my skin is the best feeling. I find a pair of slacks and a blue button down in the back of the closet and select that. I hate wearing ties, so I guess it's a good thing I can't find one. A pair of blue, black and white Jordan 1s completes the attire.

I take a quick shower and brush my teeth. I quickly get dressed and make my way downstairs to the garage. The only choice is which car I'll drive, mine or dad's. We had similar taste when it came to cars. Both of us liked blacked out vehicles. Black car, black interior, black rims, all black everything. Difference is he was a little flashier than I was.

I suppose that's the kind of man he was. 68' Pontiac GTO, perfect condition. He always had a thing for muscle cars, but this was his baby. Other cars would come and go but he kept this one, and always took care of it. Mom and I are probably the only other people who he let drive it. He always swore he could outrun anything in the car. Loud as a motorcycle and just as fast. Funny thing is he always did the speed limit. Never commit a misdemeanor while committing a felony. My car, simple, Chevy Blazer. Looks like a soccer mom with good taste is coming up the street. All the bells and whistles with a few extra features. Custom black paint job, still lowkey in any part of the city. I think I'll take my own car today.

I don't even know why I pretend to make that choice every day. I haven't had the heart to drive dad's car since I brought it here. Just doesn't feel right driving his car when nobody has faced any consequences for his death. Kind of like he still has unfinished business out there in the world.

I park on the block I grew up on, away from the actual family business. That's something dad taught me. I just need a moment for something that I know. Instead I find the whole place looks different now. Places where there used to boarded up windows are now vintage shops. Grafiti has been replaced with hand painted murals trying to mimic the style. The whole thing looks crazy. Gentrification, that shit will rip the heart right out of a community. Probably a good thing the liquor store is gone, but so are half the people that built the neighborhood. There's nobody outside selling food, fragrances or anything like that. The gentrifiers seem to think armed guards at every door is the way to go about keeping black people out of their shops. That's all it is.

I used to think my car kept attention away from me, but I'm seeing that might not be the case around here. Way too many people are starting to look and point. White people love to call the police too. I'm not holding or anything, but I don't want those problems. Time to move on.

"That you in there Javon," a knock at my passenger side window. It's Andrea, a blast from my past.

"Hey, what's going on," I roll down the passenger side window so she can see me.

"Give me a ride to the grocery store."

"You were waiting on the bus until you saw me."

"Now I want to ride with you," she reaches in and unlocks the door herself.

"Some people would shoot you for reaching in their car like that."

"Everybody knows you're not a gangster," she buckles her seatbelt with a smile.

"I am. I'm so gangster. I eat cereal without the milk," because I'm lactose intolerant.

"If you were gangster, you'd be in charge not Grady," words do hurt. I'd prefer sticks and stones.

This is why we broke up. She always had a way to cut me with just her words. She's right, I'm not really a gangster. I know that. I've been playing one ever since my dad died. Not even sure why. Pretty sure a psychologist would just say I'm trying to understand my father by becoming my father. But I think I knew him pretty well. Still that was completely uncalled for.

"Grady is in charge because I haven't taken him out yet. He'll get his."

"Because I haven't taken him out yet," she mocks me. "Boy stop, you're trying way too hard. You've got a good education and you know your parents didn't like you out in the streets. Go be a teacher or something. Out here selling drugs like you're somebody else."

I just spend the rest of the ride in silence. She tells me how everything in the neighborhood has changed. Mrs. Tyson died when they forced her to move out the home she had been in for the last fifty years. When she's done with that, she starts to chew me out again. I don't come around enough. I should be helping the community. I wasn't exactly fond of getting chewed out in my own car. Even if it was from someone I used to love, or care about a lot. She just put me in a bad mood. What makes her think she has the right to just question who I am? I'm not even mad to be honest, just trying to hype myself up. Nothing she said is completely wrong. I just didn't want to hear it from her. I've been telling myself the same thing for a while now.

"And remember, above all else, you need to be true to yourself Javon," she closes the door behind her.

I make my way to my father's grave and just kind of stare. I've never actually come out here because I don't really know what to do at someone's grave. I also never really had an urge before now. But it was on the way, so it didn't hurt to stop. People come and leave flowers, cards or their favorite foods. What good does that actually do? It isn't like they can smell the flowers, and they can't read the cards at all. I know for a fact they can't eat the food. So why do they do it? Maybe I should just talk. I see people talking all the time.

"Hey dad, I miss you. I think about you, a lot. I mean all the time. There's not really a day that goes by when you don't cross my mind," the words sound silly coming out of my mouth. "Sometimes I want to take all the pictures of you out of my house so it doesn't hurt to see them," this is dumb. I wouldn't ever say anything like this to my dad. Even if it is true, we never spoke like this. We were always straight with each other. No beating around the bush. "Look dad, at your funeral people couldn't help but say how proud of me you were. Well, I screwed it all up. You told me never be sorry, just be better. Well I'm going to fix all of this. I'm going to get everything right. Everyone said how you always worried about if you were a good father. Said you didn't have good fathers in your life as an example, and you didn't. You were the best father anyone could have. You didn't give me everything I wanted, but you made sure I could earn anything I wanted. The hard way, the right way. You were there whenever screwed up and helped me fix it. You didn't judge me for anything as long as I was happy. I didn't care about any flaws you had; you were perfect for me. I miss you. I miss all your advice. I love you."

I had so much more I wanted to say, but that's the only thing I could think of. It would have been so much easier to just say this stuff to him when he was alive. Why didn't I take that chance? I guess I have to put that behind me for now. I suppose it's time to move on with my life, be my own man. I don't even know what that really means. I guess I should figure it out.

CHAPTER 3

"Well the devil must be in tears today. Is that Little Javon Swift I see? Looking like a grown man. Give me a hug boy," Deacon Jackson wraps his arms around me tight for more of a bear hug than a church hug. "I can't believe you showed up today. Dressed for the occasion too. Even you are still wearing gym shoes to church when you're almost thirty. Shame you're a little late. But, the Lord knows you wanted to be here," he jumps right into the same speech he gives every time he sees me.

"It's good to see you too Deacon Jackson," I'm hoping he can hear the sarcasm in my voice.

"Hey young brother let me kick it with you for a second," he pulls me over to the side of the church.

"I heard you was selling that stuff now. I know your dad used to do it, but you don't need to follow in his footsteps. Apples don't fall far from the tree, but they do roll down hills. You hearing me?"

"Yes sir."

"Nah, nope. I don't think you are. I had a brother named Harold. He used to mess with that heroin," he said heroin but pronounced it hair ron, "He used to sell it, then he started using it. Whole life just in the trash messing with that mess. It ain't good for you. You ain't using it is you?"

"No sir."

"26 is too old to be messing with that junk. Either you

end up dead, or in jail. You don't get a say in the matter. Why don't you do something good and work for Jesus. Go help the young kids. Do it now, while you got a clean record. You can really help these kids," he takes my hand and puts it between both his own. Almost as if he's begging me. But he doesn't really know me, but I don't really know this man, and he doesn't really know me so his prayers fall on deaf ears.

"Javon, is that you? You missed the whole service. You know what time church starts," mom walks over at top speed.

"Sorry mom, you remember Andrea, she needed a ride to the store," I plead my case.

"I ain't worried about those hoochie mommas you roll around with, I'm sorry Deacon Jackson," she says with a crooked neck that means she isn't really sorry at all.

"Javon, it was good to see you again. Just think about what I said okay," Deacon Jackson shakes my hand runs off in fear of my mother.

"Where are you taking me for lunch," didn't even say she was happy to see me.

She knew where we were going. The only place she ever wants to go, Pete's Chicken and Chops. If we went anywhere else, she would complain. She still complained the whole way to the restaurant. Didn't like what I was wearing. My truck is too big. My truck is too small. Sneakers and suits don't go together. I was ready to be done with this lunch as soon as she started talking. But, we always went out as a family on the anniversary of her and dad meeting. It was just us now, but we still made the effort. Even if we didn't like each other much at that moment and this little retreat caused us physical pain. The moments where we do like each other are getting further and further apart.

"Oh, I get it, there's no room for black people in your restaurant," mom is so quick to play the race card. It's Sunday, after church. People rush to restaurants, like we're doing right now. There's a black family sitting ten feet from us. She just hates when she isn't the center of attention. It worked, and we got seated ahead of everyone already waiting. I hate when she does stuff like this, but it works out for her anyway. She just complains until it works out even if her complaint is just wrong.

"So how has everything been," smiling like she didn't just cause a scene.

"Fine."

"Your uncle says you haven't really been bringing in a lot. You aren't skimming off the top are you," with a raised eyebrow.

"Why would I do that?"

"It might be one of those knucklehead friends of yours."

"Nobody is skimming off the top because there is no top to skim off. Did you just want to talk work today or did you want to try being a family," half an hour is all it took for her to get under my skin.

"Okay what would you like to talk about then?"

"How was church mom?"

"It was wonderful. I really felt the spirit in there. It would be nice if you joined me sometimes."

"I'll pass on it. Not really my thing."

"What is your thing baby? Have you found your passion in life yet," she's just full of sarcasm.

"Oh, I don't know. I was thinking about going to HVAC school. Trade school seems more my pace than accounting."

"When are you going to invite me to your home Javon? You've been there almost a year and haven't invited me in at all."

"I'll have to throw a family gathering."

"That will be so wonderful. Labor Day is coming up soon," she says.

This whole conversation is so damn fake. I wanted her to just be normal like we used to be but that's kind of hard to do when the moment dad died she started fucking my uncle. Then she married him before the ink on the death certificate died.

"This whole lunch thing isn't working. We should try again later. Clearly neither of us is in the mood for this right now," I'm just trying to leave before this gets any worse.

"Well, I don't want to be around your gloomy ass either. Always acting like the world fucking hates you. You got more than most people and you always acting like you got nothing," she spits back.

"You started sleeping with my uncle before my dad was in the ground and you think I should be okay with that?"

"You should mind your own business."

"How can I mind my own business? Do you not hear people talking? It's shameful. Pathetic. It's everyone's business right now. You two are the only ones that think this is a secret."

"Ungrateful motherfucker" she reaches across the table and tries to smack me but I lean back and she misses. "After your dumb ass dropped out of school we gave you a way to survive and this is how you act?"

"You know what? Have a great meal mom. I'll see you around," I'm just leaving. I can't deal with her today.

I don't even know why I try with her sometimes. Dad always made me do what she said even when I didn't want to. She's never got anything nice to say. My whole life she just talked shit. Javon you cry too much. You're too emotional to be a real man Javon. Why is it taking you so long to graduate college Javon? You too good sell drugs? You think you're better than everyone else Javon. I don't need that shit in my life right now. I didn't need it then either. I just tolerated it. I can't do it anymore. The family events are officially through. Maybe one day we can try again, but now it's a wrap. I'll get a burger and call it a day. The phone rings and cuts off my music as soon as I pull onto the street.

"What the fuck did you say to your mother," my loud ass uncle starts yelling.

"I told her to act like a fucking adult Grady," I keep my cool. Don't need him to know I'm angry.

"You need to start showing your mother some respect."

"Did you show my father respect?"

"What are you talking about boy?"

"It's not real respectful to start fucking your dead brother's wife and move into his home before his body is in the ground. Seems like you don't know shit about respect Grady," he just breathes heavy for a moment.

"One of these days, I'm going to fuck you up. You need to be thankful your mother won't let me show you how I handle people like you."

"How do you handle people like me? You don't do shit but sit in front of a TV all day. You're not handling anything or anyone," I don't fear this man. He needs to learn that I don't respond to threats.

"Show some respect motherfucker," he hangs up. Always has to have the last word.

I need to move to LA or something. The two of them are ridiculous. Both of them are adults but think the world revolves around them. They're constantly on me trying to get me to do whatever they want. They can't even realize how messed up this situation is for everyone else. The nerve of them to act like they're being disrespected because I'm not okay with my mother screwing my uncle before my father's body is cold. Nobody would be okay with this. Both of them, just arrogant. I can't take much more of this.

CHAPTER 4

The sound of glass being tapped on lightly wakes me up. I must have fell asleep on the couch watching TV. The knocking keeps coming, it takes a minute to see where the noise is coming from. The sliding glass door in the kitchen, I always hated that thing. It's dark but I can make out a person back there knocking. They wave when they realize I'm looking at them. Nobody knows where I live but Nate and Tevin. I don't like pop up visits and it deters people who try to catch me slipping. This person looks a lot more, shapely than Nate or Tevin and they would just use the front door. The hips tell me it's a woman for sure. I've never brought any women to this place. I usually go to their place, so I can leave when it's over. I'm just not the type to get involved with long relationships. Taking trips and giving gifts just isn't my kind of thing, and I'm not a fan of excessive romance and cuddling either. So, I know for a fact that I don't know this woman.

I've never been afraid of someone coming after me, but I just like my space. Still, I know I can handle anything that walks through that door. Dad made sure I got a good education and stayed away from the streets. But he didn't raise a bitch either. I walk over to the wall and flip the switch. I watch the motion lights turn on and show her face, she wines from the sudden brightness. I don't recognize this woman at all. She's older than I am, closer to my parents' ages probably. She's got her hair in an old school Pam Grier afro, a turtleneck sweater, dress pants, but sneakers. I can't really get a read on what she's here to do. She puts her hands up and spins around to show she isn't armed with anything but a cell phone.

"Hey Javon, I just want to talk," she does that silly yelling whisper thing I hate. You aren't whispering and it just makes it harder to understand. "It's about your father."

I'm not really sure how to handle this now. She knows who I am, and I don't know her. If she keeps making noise, I'm sure the neighbors will get worried and call the police. That doesn't make things easier. Even if I don't keep anything at home, the visuals alone cause issues. She starts knocking harder as if I can't see her. I guess I don't have any choice but to let her in. I'm not doing this without any protection by my side. I make my way back to the living room, and slide open the TV stand drawer. Inside the drawer I lift a hidden slat to reveal my gun. Fully legal, just well hidden.

I make my way towards the door and make sure she sees the gun in my hand. I don't aim it, never aim at anyone or anything that you aren't ready to kill. If she gets scared that can cause more problems than a random woman outside my house. She nods accepting the situation she's in. A little too easily if you ask me. But I've never been in this situation before, I'll follow her lead even if she doesn't realize it. I close my eyes and take a few deep breaths. Just enough to calm myself down and make sure I was thinking clearly. I slide open the glass door and signal her to come in. I peak around the corner to make sure she's alone and lock the door behind me.

"It's so nice to finally meet you Javon. You look just like your father. Not as big, you don't have the same muscle mass, but just like him. Especially when we were teenagers, I'll have to dig out some pictures," she starts the conversation as if this is just a normal day.

"I've got the gun, I think I should be doing the talking."

"You're not going to shoot me. You didn't aim, and you didn't even put your finger on the trigger. That shows you've got some self-control and you're thinking this through. Smart man, just like your dad. Besides, you wouldn't want an unarmed dead cop in your home, would you? That's not a good look."

"If you're a cop, I really need you to leave. I don't speak with any police."

"Your dad did. All the time. We were good friends," she says with a smile.

"My dad wasn't a snitch," I grip the gun tighter.

"Woah, I never said all that. I just said we used to speak a lot."

"How did you know him?"

"We grew up together. We had a few flings back in the day. He was my first love. You should have seen him back then. You really look like him when he was in high school. I just can't get over that. Before he started hitting the weights anyway. We stayed in touch through the years and would meet occasionally."

"I knew all of my dad's side chicks, and you aren't one," way too uppity for dad's type. On top of that she's a cop.

"Side chick? Negro, I am way above side chick status. I'm more than that."

"Then what are you? Some stalker cop trying to build a case?"

"No. A best friend, a confidant, and a person to lean on," she sighs and takes a seat at the kitchen island as if she lives there.

"I don't believe you."

"That's fine. We really did grow up together. Best friends, life just took us in different directions. I ended up with a badge and he was on the other side of the law. Still, loyalty and being a good person is more important than cops and robbers. We had an agreement. I never wanted to go after him, so he never sold or even drove drugs through my precinct. After we settled on that, we never talked about work again unless we were venting. It worked out great until he died."

"So that's why he never wanted to expand. He didn't want to cross you. It wasn't about being greedy with the money," I didn't realize I said that out loud until she nodded.

"Javon, I need your help," she says looking into my eyes. Her own eyes have tears forming on them.

"What do you need from me," I'm not obligated to help her. But, seeing this woman cry in my kitchen bothers me enough that I want to help if I can.

"I think your uncle Grady set your father up to be killed and I,"

"Me too," I interrupt her.

"If I take this case to trial, I need you to testify about your uncle."

"Can't do it. I want him gone as much as you, but I'm not testifying," she made some bold demands as if I wouldn't be labeled a snitch the rest of my life.

"Then how do you want to do it? You want to shoot him? We can go to his house right now, shoot him and be done with it. You can do it; I don't even need to be there. I'll drive you if you promise you can pull the trigger. Javon, you don't know me, but talking to your dad, I know you. You slept with a teddy bear until you were fifteen, you're not a killer. I've seen you out there trying to sell drugs. You're terrible at it. This street shit isn't for you. It isn't what your dad wanted for you either."

"You don't know anything about me. You think you know some stories, but you never met me."

"I do my research. How do you think I found this house? I know your best friends. I know you studied accounting in college but dropped out because you were close to failing anyway. I know your license plate number.

I know you never got a ticket. I know you claim not to eat fast food, but you order a bacon jalapeño spicy chicken sandwich and large chili once a week at Wendy's. I know a lot about you, I'm a detective. I detect shit. One thing is, you aren't built for the drug game. Hell, your best friend Nathaniel isn't built for it either. Maybe even less than you. You want street justice? But you aren't going to deliver it. Your gun is registered, you don't take it out the house and you've never even threatened to shoot someone. I know you. Testifying is all you've got as a way to get back at Grady."

"Get the fuck out of my house," I say opening the door again.

"Okay, I'll leave my card. Think about it," I don't accept the card. I let it fall to the floor instead. Never taking my eyes off her.

"One last question. How did you find me?"

"I told your dad I would watch out for you. I'm not going to give up how I found you that easily."

"Next time you come to my house, I'll shoot you."

"No, you won't," she laughs at me as she exits.

I don't know how much of what she said was true, but she sounded convincing. She just knew way too much about me. If what she was saying is true, she knew a lot about dad too. I don't know if what she was saying about dad is true. But I doubt she could do that much research on a dead man. I'd ask mom about her but based on the way she was talking mom wouldn't have any clue about this.

My life is a mess right now. Mom is mad at me. I got an uncle breathing down my neck wanting me to break. I'm not making any money. Now, I've got a woman claiming to be a cop showing up at my door telling me she used to get down with my dad. She wants me to testify in court. The house I thought was a secret, is apparently easy to find. Who could live a life like this and not go crazy? Javon Swift, I hope.

CHAPTER 5

"Hey, I got money this time," Kevin yells when he sees Tevin stepping off the steps to meet him again.

"You really do," Tevin is shocked as Kevin waves a crisp twenty-dollar bill.

"Javon, I heard your uncle is mad as hell. What you do," Kevin couldn't just get his fix and go.

"I didn't do anything Kevin."

"You did something, Javon," Kevin is rolling his neck at me and emphasizing my name.

"Kevin, go ahead and get moving," Tevin tells him, and Kevin walks off happy. "Why are we still sitting here not making any money," he asks taking his seat.

"Do you have a better idea? Because I don't," I've got enough on my mind right now.

Tevin and Nate start to go over ideas and I keep thinking back to last night. How would this woman know who I was? I've got almost every photo my father and I took when he was living. I don't have a criminal record and he wasn't on any of my college papers. Maybe she did know him. I could have dreamed it all. I fell asleep watching TV for sure. Who's to say I didn't dream an episode of a cop show or something.

"Robbing drug dealers doesn't make you some kind of Black Robin Hood," Nate throws his hands up.

"Well, what do you think Javon," Tevin turns to me.

"I missed the question. What were we talking about?"

"Maybe if you didn't spend all night playing with yourself, you could stay awake," Tevin laughs at his own joke.

"I was playing with your momma. Now what were we talking about?"

"Only person momma getting played with around here is your momma, by your," Tevin starts

"He was saying," Nate interrupts before he can finish. "He thinks we should rob some dealers and take their money. He's got this whole plan about how it would work. He thinks it'll be like a movie. We get some silencers then we kick in the front door and just start firing. You shoot anyone that tries to run out the back. We take their money and run. Stolen cars so they can't trace us."

"First, I'm not shooting anyone over some money, second this isn't a movie. Last thing, that is probably the stupidest thing you have ever said. This is why you never get to come up with any of our plans. Thinking, is not your strong point. But you're good in other ways," always end with a compliment.

"So what do you got then college boy," Tevin asks crossing his arms.

"I got nothing. It's homecoming weekend, let's just hope someone decides they want something harder than weed. Because that little plan you got, is stupid," I stand up and stretch. "Nate what you got?"

"Nothing, Nate never has anything," Tevin starts.

"Ignore, him. What you got Nate?"

"Well, I was thinking. You said you wanted to branch out a couple of days ago. Sell something that people were actually buying. We could do that. Like you said, it's homecoming weekend. People are going to be looking for good stuff. We could be the ones that give it to them," Nate speaks looking down at the ground, not really sure of his own plan.

"What did you have in mind," I ask before Tevin can

interrupt.

"Well, weed is always popular. But, college kids like pills and stuff now. We can get a few different kinds of pills. Hit up a few different parties and work the crowd. Javon, I know you can find us some parties. That's your thing. Cops won't be checking for drugs, because it'll be worth more trouble than the arrests. We just stay clear of places they're working security and leave if something gets started. I know a guy I used to buy weed from. He sells a lot of other stuff too. Good prices, never said where he gets it. But, I don't think he's a cop or anything like that. Nobody has ever had a problem with him. I can give him a call and see how much he can sell us. He might even be willing to front it as long as you guys play it cool when we go for the pickup."

It's a good plan. Nate comes up with some great plans when he isn't stuck in his own head or letting Tevin get to him. Just about anything is better than what we're doing now, which amounts to a whole lot of nothing. I wonder how long Nate has been thinking about this. Knowing him, he's had it on his mind for a while. Glad he finally shared.

"Damn, that might just work out. Make the call," I smile giving Nate my approval and he fumbles rushing to grab his phone. "I'll go grab my truck."

When I make it back to the spot all the joy is gone from Nate's face and Tevin is smiling. I would say I love Tevin like a brother at this point, but he's just an asshole. I don't even need to ask what he did. I know he said something messed up to Nate. He just can't let anyone else have a moment in the sun, because he wants to be Black Rambo or something. He reaches for the front seat and I keep the door locked.

"Nate, you ride up front. It's your plan, and I need directions. Tevin sit in the back," I unlock the door and watch Tevin push past Nate to get in the back.

Along the way Nate fills me in on what he knows about

this guy. Doesn't have any ties to anyone in the game. Nate started buying weed from him back when I was away in college. Met him at a nightclub, he was working the room. This was before Nate started selling with Tevin. The guy gets his stuff from different suppliers. Nate could never figure out where he got the pills, but he had an infinite supply of them and could get anything with no problem. He always offered them to Nate but Nate wasn't fond of popping pills. Nate smokes weed, but beyond that, he pretty much avoids drugs and alcohol. That's how I met him back at a party in a high school. The party didn't have any bud, and I wasn't going to stay around, because that's my only vice. He felt the same way, and asked for a ride. We spent the rest of the night smoking and laughing. Turns out we knew a lot of the same people. Like, goofy ass Tevin.

The further we get out of the city, the more nervous I get. I thought this would be some guy on the other side of the city, but we're outside the city limits now. We've been driving for about forty-five minutes. We're out in the suburbs now, but Nate is sure we're heading towards the right place. We finally stop at a small pink house on the corner. A nice Mercedes parked in the driveway and freshly trimmed lawn. Kids are playing outside. This is not the place I expected to be buying a bunch of drugs at. Nate swears we're in the right place, this is his mission, so I let him take lead. I have to because Tevin won't shut the fuck up.

"Tevin watch the truck," Nate has got his confidence back.

"I'm not watching the truck in the suburbs. What's the worst thing that could happen? Some kids scratch it with a bike," I'm glad Tevin is upset. This is how he treats everyone else anyway.

"Well stay in the truck then. Don't need your hot head on this one," I exit the truck followed by Nate.

Tevin doesn't get out, but I turn the alarm on. Just to

fuck with him. Nate and I burst out in laughter. We can't see his face because of the tinted windows, but we know he's pissed off in there. That's part of the fun. We head up to the door and Nate knocks and a man's voice calls from the inside. A man answers the door in pajama bottoms and no shirt. He's standing about seven feet tall with platinum blonde hair. He greets Nate like an old friend and welcomes us inside before leading us to a back room. His name is AC but all I'm thinking is Sisqo'neil. The love child of Sisqo and Shaq is selling us drugs in the suburbs, what kind of make-believe world am I living in right now?

I play my part and joke around every now and then to keep the mood light while Nate brokers the deal. It's a role I've never seen him in, but he does a good of negotiating. He's tough on how much we're going to kick back to AC. Nate really had been thinking about this for a while. Otherwise he wouldn't have been so prepared. I'm impressed by this all. Soon a deal is in place and we all shake hands on it.

"Not that it's any of my business, but you're letting us take ten thousand dollars' worth of pills on consignment. Even then, you're still giving us a friend discount. How can you afford this," I can't help but ask, it'll bother me if I didn't.

"I have a connect. The drugs get delivered to a hospital near here. Not even on the official record. The hospital pays for them. Never see them, never even realize they paid. Doesn't cost me any money at all," AC shrugs like that isn't crazy to consider.

"Who is giving you this many pills for free," I ask, much to Nate's displeasure.

"I didn't say free. It doesn't cost me money. But you know the saying, this dick ain't free," we all laugh at the joke. That's enough to put me at ease.

As we're leaving a white man in pink scrubs with pink hair gets out of a pink car parked in the driveway. He's carrying a backpack similar to the one AC handed us the pills in. He switches up to the door and opens it with a key. From outside, we hear him yell out for his baby. The two of us burst out in laughter. Suddenly, the pink house makes a lot of sense and we know who his plug is.

CHAPTER 6

"Are we really doing this," Tevin asks with a pocket full of pills like he isn't already committed.

"Yep," that's all I've got for him this time. I just don't have the energy for him.

"So where's this party," Nate changes the topic before Tevin can start having another fit.

"We're going to a warehouse over by some train tracks, just before you get to downtown. It's going to be a gangster rave."

"What's that," they ask in unison. I was confused when I heard it for the first time too.

"It's a rave, but instead of techno or whatever, they listen to gangster rap from the 90s."

"That sounds stupid," I expected that from Tevin, but it was Nate.

"Yeah, I think so too. But white people love them, black hipsters love them and they all love drugs and proving they have lots of money. We just so happen to have drugs, and need lots of money. So, let's go get these hipsters fucked up," I feel like I'm giving the same pep talk that every dealer gives in a movie when police have just raided the spot.

We split up the rest of our pills and head towards the front door. The doorman picks up on us right away, assuming we're up to no good. We are up to no good, but he didn't have to pull us to the side like that. Tevin tried playing the tough guy but it's hard to be the tough guy when you're looking at some 6'5 linebacker who moonlights as a bouncer. Nate was ready to duck and cover, but I had a plan.

"How much will it cost you to look the other way and tell us if the cops are coming," straight to the point. The dollar rules everything and I doubt he cares more about this club than he does cash in hand.

"Five hundred if you want me to keep quiet and play lookout," the security guard doesn't beat around the bush. He's done this before.

"How do you know we'll make that much," Nate adds his thoughts to the price.

"Y'all walked up laughing and joking. Clearly this isn't a hustle or starve situation. It's not my first rodeo. I'll take five hundred," It'll be better to pay this guy, keep him on our side. He's done this before.

"Alright, I'll give you two hundred now, and three when we leave tonight," pops always said don't give up all the money up front.

"I can work with that," he takes the money and lets us walk right in without a search or anything.

"Let's split up, meet outside when it starts to die down," I have to repeat myself a few times so they can hear me over the music.

This place is crazy, nothing like the parties I went to when I was in college. Then again, I didn't party with a bunch of rich white kids trying to be down for the culture. I didn't party with a lot of black kids who were afraid to visit their cousins in the hood either. Who could even afford to rent out a warehouse for the night? The song choices are a little odd. There's no real flow to the songs being played and the DJ isn't really mixing anything, just playing the next track. I wasn't sure how they were going to have a rave with gangster rap. Never thought I would hear Snoop Dogg and Skrillex at the same time. I think its trash but the people seem to love it. They've got some crazy lighting going and there's a machine spitting out bubbles from somewhere. They spent a lot of money on this party, that means there's a lot of money to be made in here tonight.

Nate is surprising me again, he's been full of them lately. I know it was his plan, he has to be all in, but wow. He's moving through the crowd and socializing with people. If I don't pick a spot to set up shop he's going to make me look bad. I've never been good at dealing, but he's worse than I am. At least I thought he was, turns out he just needed the right spot. Tevin, not so much. He sticks out like a sore thumb; he never knows how to play it cool. In a crowd where nobody is fighting or shit talking, he's a fish out of water. A different breed, kicking in doors would have worked for Tevin, but not me and definitely not Nate.

As for me, this place reminds me of why I hated college so much. Even before I started failing classes. Everyone is partying and having a good time, but you can still smell the arrogance in the air. A bunch of people who think they're better than everyone else because they're part of some legacy family, got daddy's money or they're the acceptable black friend. I don't hate these people, but I hate being around them. It drains me, and they always expect you to kiss their asses. That was the worst part of college for me, the people. I just didn't have the energy to deal with them when pops died. I had to leave before I threw someone through a window or choked out a teacher.

"You rolling," I lean in close and ask a scruffy looking white guy who is in the middle of scouting the party.

"Nah, not yet," he yells over the music.

"You want to get started now?"

"Hell yeah, what you got" he says, eyes lighting up.

"Anything you need a prescription for, I got."

I pass him a couple pills for free. The first one is always free, a trash rule. But, if you give someone a free high, they'll think it was the best high ever. Then they'll tell all their friends. I pick a corner with a couple of arm chairs and take a seat. I can see the whole room from here and it isn't far from an emergency exit. Just in case our security friend doesn't actually warn us that there's going to be some police coming. Not that I expect them, they're probably busting up some house party with cheap liquor and a little bit of weed. This isn't the kind of people they usually go after.

It takes a while but people start coming to see me. The pills are moving way faster than crack ever did. I don't think I've even sold twenty rocks in the year I've been doing it, so they weren't exactly moving fast. I'm sure I got shorted on cash a couple of times tonight. But I've got enough to pay for the drugs with just my earnings for the night. The bigger issue is I'm getting the pills mixed up. I'm forgetting which ones are which. I don't want to be responsible for someone overdosing because I mixed up a Percocet and an Oxycodone. Luckily, hipster drug addicts are really picky about their drugs and quick to correct me. You can't just treat them like you treat Kevin back on the block, they'll let you know your service as a drug dealer is not five-star rated. The good thing is they've got way more money to spend and will pay just about anything for their drugs. I've been raising the price all night and nobody is questioning it. I know Nate and Tevin are somewhere in the crowd but I can't see how well they're doing. Nate is probably raising prices too, but Tevin might not be smart enough to do that without one of us telling him.

"Hey Mr. Big Shot," a blonde woman slurring her speech starts to talk to me.

"What you need?"

"I need some of that BBC," she giggles before she starts to dry heave.

"Lot of BBC out there, I'm sure someone will help you out," but anyone who says BBC non-ironically will never get the time of day from me.

She starts to talk again but dry heaves some more

before burping. The smell of liquor fills my personal space, and I'm quickly moving from annoyed to pissed off. She's had enough to drink for both of us. She starts to dry heave again, but this time it isn't dry. She covers her mouth and rolls her eyes back into her heard. Now I'm about to help this crazy white girl. I grab her by the arm and lead her to the bathroom around the corner. I skip the line and take her into the men's room. The guys vacate thinking some nasty bathroom sex is about to go down. She rushes into a stall and starts to vomit.

"Aren't you going to hold my hair," she manages to ask me this between bouts of vomiting.

"No."

I flip her hair away from the toilet but refuse to hold it as she finishes emptying her stomach. A few guys wander in curious to see what was going on. I lock eyes with one, he instantly recognizes that I don't want to be in this situation and tosses his hands up as if he's been in this spot before. I'm grateful for his sympathy until I hear everyone laughing outside the door.

"Yo, are you good," I ask her as she sits on the floor.

"I'm good, let me make sure you're good now," she grabs at my zipper. I'm not sure how she's still drunk. I just watched her throw up everything in her body.

"Yeah, I'm already good. You have a good night."

She grips my leg with more strength than I would expect her tiny frame to have as I tried to walk out. I just snatch my leg away from her and keep walking. I don't intend on having sex with any drunk women. Especially not a drunk white woman in a dimly lit bathroom. I'll pass. The year is 2019 and the Klan has risen again. I'm not about to go out like George Ward.

"Hey bro, she good to go another round," some guy asks me on my way out.

"She's not good to go any rounds, and I'm not your bro."

I don't want to deal with this woman any more but I

head back to the bathroom and walk her to a bench in the corner with a bottle of water to sober up. At least now I can sleep well knowing I didn't leave her there to be taken advantage of. That's my good deed for the night. I've still got a few more pills to sell and she's derailed me for long enough. I make my way back to the other side of the party and chill out. The sales trickle in now as the party starts to die down. Still enough people that I can unload the rest of my product.

I head out through the front and offer the other half of our little bribe to the security guard. He declines, turns out Nate finished up way before I did. He's already paid the guard and spent his time parking lot pimping, at least trying anyway. Tevin makes it out last. He looks like he's been drained of everything he has and seen way more than he ever wanted, but he sold everything he had tonight. We made a killing tonight without even counting. It's a good time to be alive.

"Hey, you the boys who been selling on my turf," some short pasty guy with a Fall Out Boy haircut approaches us yelling.

"You think we sell drugs because we're black," Nate has jokes tonight, and we all crack up laughing.

"I want a cut, so how much you got," this guy is really not backing down. Does he think this is a movie? I mean we're drug dealers, real dealers. Not just some rich kids playing the part.

"Hey, how old are you," I can't help but ask.

"I'm nineteen but that doesn't matter," oh, he's just a kid to me.

"You got a gun kid," I ask with a smile. I know he doesn't.

"No."

"Okay, Tevin, give him what we've got for him," I smile at Tevin.

"For real? You want me to give it to him," Tevin is surprised that we're on the same page tonight.

"Hell yeah, hand it over," the kid just keeps talking.

"Alright, it's right here," Tevin says digging deep into the crotch of his jeans.

I already know where this is going and I can feel the smile stretch across my face. I just didn't think Tevin would be so theatrical with it. He digs his hand all around his crotch before pulling it from his pants and smelling it. He shakes his head at his own funk. Nate and I are already laughing but the kid still doesn't know what's about to happen to him. Just another sign that we aren't the same. When Tevin stretches his arm back behind his own shoulder the kid's eyes light up. He realizes a little too late, as he moves to block, Tevin's hand comes across his face at full speed in an open hand slap. Our laughter amplifies as he falls to the ground from an open hand slap.

"Now, what you got little man," Tevin asks crouching down to look into his face.

☐

CHAPTER 7

Tonight, was a good night. We made some money, Tevin beat a guy up. We had some good street tacos at a food truck afterwards. We're pretty good drug dealers if we put our minds to it. Still, I don't want to do this. I can't go play accountant either but selling drugs, is not the life for me. Dad always wanted to go legit, that was the whole point of the accounting thing. Maybe I could go start a business or something. I'm not sure what kind. Probably start buying a couple of gas stations. I can't cook a lot of different things, so a restaurant is out of the question. Corner stores just lead to selling more drugs eventually. Property might be the best option for me. I could just learn to fix stuff, chill out and collect some money.

The car behind me blows the horn to let me know I should go. I must have spaced out for a moment stop light. I didn't realize the light had turned green already. I'm tired, it's been a good day, but a long one. I hear police sirens behind me and immediately check my speed. Thirty-eight, the speed limit is forty so I should be good. I pull over to the side of the road with another car and wait for the officer to pass. Instead he pulls in behind me and steps out. He waves the other driver off and steps up to my window.

"Do you know why I stopped you," he asks as if I already know the answer.

"No sir," I try to play it cool and respectful. As respectful as I can knowing he's already made up his mind on how this stop will go.

"You were speeding and swerving in a school zone boy," he says chewing on a toothpick.

"It isn't during school hour sir," this is a set up. I'm not going to lose my cool.

"Why are you questioning me? Have you had anything to drink tonight?"

"No sir."

"I need your license and registration."

I move towards my glove box to grab my registration. He coaxes me to take it easy and not to move too quickly. All the while, he's smiling. He's making it sound as if he's fearing for his life. In reality, he's getting a kick out this whole situation. I guess he's having the good night now. He takes my license and registration and heads back to his car. I sit and wait. There's nothing. I've never been arrested. My car is registered to me and only me. My license and registration are both clean. I move my hand to check my phone before he speaks over the loudspeaker.

"Mr. Swift, I need you to keep your hands on the wheel," he's just being an asshole now.

I've never been stopped by a police officer before, but I know it doesn't take this long to run a license and registration. On cue he steps from his vehicle and makes his way back up to me.

"Looks like you've got a clean record. But you were still swerving. I'm going to need you to step out so I can search you for narcotics," he licks his lips like he's gotten me.

"I don't consent to a search."

"I didn't ask you boy."

"I know my rights."

"I don't give a damn about your rights. There was a time when my grandfather was an officer of the law. He would have just pulled you from the car and beat you. Be lucky, I'm giving you the benefit of the doubt. Now get the fuck out the car."

I can't really respond in the fashion I want. He's got his hand on his gun now and it's out of the holster. I'm at his mercy. Still, I wonder if I can start my car and drive off before he can shoot me. I doubt it, could be worth a shot. I've got a few thousand dollars' worth of drug money tucked in the center console. I know if he searches the car, I'm going to jail. Just for suspicion of dealing. Either that, or he just kills me and takes the money for himself. I don't know what to do. I wonder if that kid Tevin smacked called the cops. Every bone in my body wants to fight right now and I can't do shit because some trigger-happy racist got a gun and a badge so now he thinks he's got a right to take my life.

"I'm not going to ask you again, step out the car, boy," this time he's waved the gun around below his belt a little. As if I couldn't already see it.

I open the car door and step out. He walks me to the squad car and I assume the position. This is the first time I've ever even been searched by a police officer. He kicks my legs apart until I'm almost doing the splits. He starts to pat me down. It's more aggressive than a search. Really, they're just aggressive pats. I cough a little as he smacks my testicles. He gets a laugh out of that. He's enjoying this.

"Why don't you wait here while I search the car boy," he walks off with like a happy school kid on his way to my car.

I'm still trying to think of a way out of this. He's a little out of shape. I could outrun him for sure. But, he's spent all this time trying to provoke me. If I take off running I know he's just going to shoot me in the back. What's the worst thing that could happen? I don't have any drugs in the car. I've got money, but a lot of people ride around with money. I don't trust bank accounts and just did some manual labor and got paid under the table. That's my story. I built a fence.

"Aww shit boy, I was going to plant some drugs on you

but this wad of money says I don't need to," he comes back with my cut of the money being held up for display.

"That's mine," I'm done cooperating.

"What kind of drugs do you sell?"

"I don't sell drugs."

"Bullshit, then how did you get it?"

"I won it at a casino. Can I have my money back?"

"No, you can't have my money."

"I want my money," I step forward to show him I mean business.

He sits the money down and walks up to me. I don't back down, he's not a cop right now. He's just a crook. We stare eye to eye. I don't expect the baton to my gut until it hits me. The air is instantly gone from my body. Before I can react, another blow comes to my back which drops me to my knees. I try to take big breaths. I don't have the air to get back on my feet right now. This time a kick to my ribs tosses me over onto my back.

"Hey, Mr. Swift, I want to apologize for any misunderstanding we had earlier. I'm Officer Sam Flagg. I ran your name, only thing I got was a mention of you in an obituary. Turns out your daddy died. By some miracle, he was one of the city's biggest drug dealers. Car full of money, seems like you took after your daddy. Well, I'm going to be taking some of that for making me beat you. I'm just going to take a little more money as a signing bonus. A show of good faith, you can keep the rest. We can help each other out. I'll just hold on to this license too. They're cheap, you can afford a replacement. See you soon Mr. Smith. I'll be in touch."

"Fuck you, give me my money," I manage to shout after him.

He doesn't take it well. He starts to lay into me with more punches and kicks. I try to cover up, but I don't have the energy after a few blows. He's done this before. He doesn't strike me in the head. Nowhere that visible wounds could be seen. I can't even be sure how long he beats me for. Eventually he spits on me and just leaves me on the side of the road.

I can get up, but I don't want to. I'm just stuck in this mud, because that's where I belong. Did I really just get beat up by some random ass cop? I didn't even fight back. I see it on the news every day but damn, did it really just happen to me? This is fucked up. On top of that, he took most of my money. Worse, he knows where I live now. I thought I would be able to get out the drug game and call it a life. Now I'm being held hostage by some crooked ass cop.

I have to kill a cop. That's the only way out. How do I kill a cop? Where do I even find him? Is Sam Flagg even a real name? This is so fucked up. I can't tell anyone about this. I have to get away. Just pack up and pretend none of this happened.

CHAPTER 8

Damn, damn, damn. I can't believe I let this happen to me. As soon as the garage door closes behind me, I sprint into my house. I have to clean this place out. I grab the to go bags I had packed in case something like this ever happened. Dad always told me to keep one packed. A lot of cash, my passport, some clothes, toothpaste, deodorant, a book and other essentials I'll need to stay off the streets for a while. I guess I'll finally get to read Hamlet or The Count of Monte Christo.

Next, I grab the important things, things that shouldn't be left in the house. My guns and a few extra magazines. I might actually need them if that cop finds me. I grab another duffel bag and head to the garage. I open the fuse box and a flip the switches in order. A click lets me know I did it right and I pull the handle revealing a hidden safe. More money, dad left so much money and almost nobody knows about most of it. My mom and uncle claimed what they knew about. There was so much they didn't know about. I gave a large chunk to side chicks and loyal friends of his, then just kept the rest. There was just so much of it. I didn't know what to do with it all. Most of it is still hidden away in places around the city. Staring at it, I could have spent it on finishing college. I just didn't want to. I spent it on a truck, and this house. I don't even have to sell drugs. I can go be a bus driver or something. I prefer not to use the money for some reason, but this is an emergency. I add the cash to the bottom of the bags and close the safe.

The cop knows my car, so I load everything into the trunk of dad's and drive out the garage slowly. I make sure nothing seems suspicious. Once I hit the end of the block I floor it and make my way across the city. If a cop tries to stop me now, I'm just not pulling over. They can't catch me. I'm sure of it. Still, I just need to make my way to the storage unit and make sure everything is locked down. Admittedly, I was greedy. I knew which stashes my mom and were hitting in their little takeover. I just made sure to hit them first. To hide the money from them I bought a storage unit and dumped it all there. I didn't know what else to do with it. If I make it through this thing with the cop, I'll make sure I find a way to invest the money safely, to help other people. There's probably close to a million in the storage unit, but I don't really know how to wash drug money. That's why I was going to be an accountant.

The storage unit looks untouched, just like I left it. Filled with a bunch of junk that means nothing to anyone. Stuff I got at different thrift stores to fill it up. I slide to the back of the room and locate the big metal lockers. A wall of lockers in a storage unit, that's all I could come up with. Dad was paranoid, panic rooms hidden all over the house and his favorite spots. Nearly every place he stored money was some overthought puzzle that nobody would be able to figure out unless he told you. Even the house I bought was a secret stash house of his at one point. Money and guns everywhere, more than any man would ever need. Now most of it was sitting right here. I suddenly understand why he was so paranoid, but in the end what good is paranoia if you don't act on it? Even if you act on it, when your time comes you don't have any choice but to surrender.

I suddenly feel too many people are watching me right now, even if it's just me and this storage unit. I pick a hotel downtown and book a reservation before leaving the storage unit. I don't really like hotels, but for now, I don't want to be at home. I got an uncle that's on my ass and watching my every move. I've got a woman who says she's a cop and knows my dad that's been stalking me. Now, I've got a crooked cop with my address, that's already robbed me and who has a hunger for more. What the fuck?

"Ah, we didn't expect you to arrive so soon Mr. Swift. If you would like to have a seat in the lobby we'll put a rush on getting your suite prepared," the front desk clerk apologizes while dialing up the housekeepers.

"How are you doing tonight honey," a woman in a green cocktail dress, pumps that are too high for her a crooked blond wig and makeup about two shades lighter than her own skin greets me. I can tell the honey is forced, and I know where this is going.

"I'm doing fine," I take a seat in an armchair.

"Seems like you could use a little company," she says taking a seat next to me. She keeps the fake country accent going.

"I'll pass on the invitation," I refuse the offer.

"Well, my name is Nicki and here's my business card if you decide to change your mind. Rates are on the back. For you, the first one is free since you're cute," she hands me her card and makes her way to the bar. Classy. I don't think prostitution is her thing. She's the only prostitute I've ever seen with a business card and a fake country accent, who is she fooling? She did smell nice, cocoa butter and vanilla, a lot better smelling than most prostitutes, and better smelling for sure. Still, not a prostitute.

Upstairs in my room I take a long shower and order room service. The whole world is turning upside down for me. More than it already was anyway. I don't know what I'm supposed to do. I would usually call my dad for something like this. If he didn't have an answer, he would at least let me talk until I found an answer for myself.

That's what I really need right now. Someone who can just talk with me. I can't call Nate on this one, he would panic too much. I could call Tevin, but he'd just want to shoot everyone. He's never shot anyone before, but it isn't like he hasn't been trying. I don't know what's wrong with him.

I laugh to myself as I grab Nicki's card form the coffee table in my suite. I flip the card and take a look at what she offers. Massages, cleaning, grocery shopping, babysitting and talking. I thought she was a prostitute to be honest. None of these things seem remotely sexual. That's good, because I didn't know if I had spiraled down enough that I was hiring prostitutes to fuck the sadness away. I guess I'll give her a call, just to chat for a little.▢

CHAPTER 9

"Javon, my man, come on in," AC greets me.

"What's going on AC."

"Same old thing, you didn't bring Nate with you this time?"

"Nah, he had some other stuff to take care of."

"How do you know I won't take advantage of you without him," he's joking but I don't know if he's talking about the pill prices or sexually. I just laugh at the joke. He has a way of speaking in double entendres, I don't know if he's playing with homophobia or just being an asshole.

"You're a good dude. You wouldn't do that," I joke handing him a backpack full of money.

"That's who you least expect to do it that betray you," He starts to count.

He's old school, counts by hand, no machines. Whoever taught him the game, was someone with a few decades in the game. AC really has turned out to be a blessing for us. Doesn't ask questions, always a nice and cordial guy. I think he might have a little crush on Tevin, which is why he stopped coming with us for the drops. Tevin isn't afraid to get shot but a little affection scares him right off. Wish I had known that a long time ago. Would have gave him some hugs or been nicer to him since that's what scares him away.

"Alright, all the money is here. I've got your next

shipment ready to go," he passes me a bag. I peak inside and feel around.

"Seems good to me," I zip the bag.

"You know, you are the only one who doesn't count every single pill. I might short you one of these days for real," AC jokes.

"Trust goes a long way in this business or any business really. "

"Trust goes a long way in life. Sometimes it's hard to figure out who you can trust," the joking tone is gone from his voice. Now more reflective, as if he's thinking about betrayals.

"AC, do you plan to do this forever or do you have an exit plan," I couldn't help but ask.

"I think about it sometimes, opening up a bakery as crazy as that sounds. I always enjoyed baking. Dad said it was for bitches. I still want to do it sometimes," he leans back on the couch and looks out the window.

"What's stopping you?"

"Nothing but myself. I got the cash; I even got a business plan. Just keep hearing about how...furious my family was when they found out I was gay. I moved here to get away from it all. Still can't get away from it. What about you Mr. Inquisitive? What's your trauma that you're running from? What's your exit plan? Since we're sharing now," he turns his attention back to me.

"I don't know yet. I just know that I don't want to do this much longer. My exit plan anyway. I'm good to go whenever, but I know Nate has been saving up to exit, so I wanted to make sure he was good."

"You growing a conscience on me?"

"Been had one, just took it a minute to turn back on," I joke with him.

"What did you want to be when you were a kid."

"Trevete," I laugh at my own joke.

"What is that?"

"Like Walker Texas Ranger, but he was the black one,"

I laugh harder.

"What is wrong with you," AC finally laughs being in on the joke. "Well, as long as you don't have a record, you can still be a cop. I won't tell that you bought drugs from me. Who expects a gay plug anyway," AC laughs at his own joke and lights a cigarette. "So, what childhood trauma keeps you up at night? I told you about my family."

"I feel like my mom never loved me. Just a means to an end. If she didn't need me for something, she didn't want me around. But at the same time, always tried to keep me caged up. Metaphorically, not a real cage. That would be messed up on some other levels."

"It's the same thing. You felt like you couldn't ever please her. Like you were just running on a treadmill that keeps getting faster until you fly off and bust through a wall."

"Just like that."

We spend another hour laughing and joking about our younger selves. Drug dealing is a club of its own, a club where most of us hate each other. But every now and then, you find a friend. I'd call AC a friend for sure. I see why Nate spoke so highly of him. We share stupid ideas we had of what it'd be like as an adult. Everybody has some idea of who they want to be when they're older. Some idea of how they'll change the world or be the best that's ever done it. Life always has other plans. AC used to be a basketball player, played in college, was headed to the NBA. Then he got accused of raping a woman. That's when he had to tell everyone he was gay to prove he was innocent. Had to give a list of men he slept with, answer invasive questions about how often and where, how he was hiding it. Then nobody wanted him to play for their team. He dropped out and had few odd jobs before he started selling drugs. Thought he was well respected, someone tried to kill him, shot his boyfriend. In another world, he could have gone pro and I could have been his accountant. But life had other plans for both of us.

I had to finally leave when I got a call from my uncle. He wants to meet with me later. Probably something about how I'm a failure and a letdown. Doesn't really matter what he thinks anyway. He's not going to kill me because that might make mom mad and he's not going to turn me into the police because I know too much. What can he really do to me?

For now, I check on my house. I've been watching the security cameras from my phone back at the hotel, but I haven't seen anyone pop in. That doesn't mean nobody has, it just means they weren't caught on camera. I take my gun and holster from the glove box. I've been carrying a gun lately because things have gotten way too weird lately. I even bought a holster for it because I didn't like tucking a gun in my waistband. I head up to my doorstep and unlock the front door, slowly opening it. I gently close it behind me and pull out my gun. Slowly I do a onceover of the house, and make sure it's clear. Nobody has been here. Everything is just as I left it. Which is bad, because I didn't take out the trash. It still isn't safe to return home. I might need to sell the house, even if I really like it. I was going to have a pool installed one day.

After I clear any food that has gone bad from the fridge and take out the trash I head over to my uncle's office. Can he call it an office? He rents a storefront in a strip mall. It used to be a tax prep shop so he left everything set up as an office. There's even a little conference room in the back. The place is there for appearances only. He really thinks he's some big shot but if the police walked in they would know the place was a drug front immediately. He's dumb enough to keep money, drugs and guns all over the building, nothing hidden at all.

"Grady, where you at," I holler from the front desk ignoring this week's fake receptionist that he's banging.

"In the back," he yells back as she scrunches up her face. Annoyed he indulged my antics.

I make my way to the back and he's got an open brick of cocaine, and a gun sitting on the desk. Does he think he's Scarface or something?

"Close the door," he growls like he's trying to show me he's scared.

"What's going on," I take a seat.

"I know you're skimming off the top."

"Off the top of what?"

"The product. You stepping on my work?"

"You give us everything already packaged up for sale. I can't even cook crack. I'd be better off selling just the cocaine. Now tell me, how would I step on it?"

"Where you getting more money at," he asks putting his hand on the gun.

"What makes you think I have more money," I ask leaning in.

"You been smelling yourself too much lately. That means you either got some new money or you got some new pussy. Considering both the bitches you run with are men, I can assume you ain't get no pussy. Unless a little man butt is what you like. I know some niggas that fuck their enemies in the ass when they catch them. Weird ass niggas. Wouldn't put it past you and your booty bandits. So, where's my money," the homophobia in that probably wouldn't have bothered me before I sat with AC and learned about his life. Now I just wonder what the point of any of that tirade was. He leans back gripping the gun waiting for answer because I've taken too long.

"You're not getting anything more than you already get from me. You set us up to fail. We found a new way to get paid. You aren't getting a cut. You want us to bring you more money? Set us up for something bigger and stop being greedy," I lean back in my seat as well. He's trying to play calm, but I actually am.

"We'll see about that," he threatens as there's a knock at the door.

"Mr. Swift," the receptionist calls from the doorway.

"What," both Grady and I respond. He doesn't get to claim the rights to my family name. His real last name is Woods. He's a bastard child, pops told me that.

"Boy, you're trying my patience. If I didn't love your mother so much," he threatens me.

"The guest are starting to arrive for the coalition meeting," she quickly says and exits the room.

"So what's on the table for tonight," I ask Grady. The coalition is more important than any beef we have.

"Nothing for you."

"What do you mean?"

"You're not invited to this meeting."

"I've been at every meeting before," I stand up to challenge this decision.

"As one of your dad's books guy. You aren't my books guy. You aren't my security. You aren't part of my team so take your narrow ass home and figure out where my money is," Grady stands up and slams his hands on the desk but the way he uttered the word books bothered me most of all.

"My dad built this coalition. Without him, you all would be shooting at each other's kids."

"Well your dad isn't here anymore. I'm in charge and if you don't change your tone, I'm going to shoot his kid."

"I would wish for someone to shoot you in the head and end it all, but that would be too quick for you. I hope nothing but bad things in life happen to you from now on, because you deserve them. Live a full life full of shit Grady," I get halfway out the door before he calls out to me.

"See there he is. The Javon I know. Throws a tantrum when he doesn't get his way. Suddenly starts talking like a white boy when he's mad. That's the real you. Go be a nurse or some shit. You ain't built for this. As hard as you think you are, I'm harder. You ain't shit but a college dropout who half-assed slings rocks and lives off the money his daddy left him. You never been your own man.

Never will be because you don't have the balls to do it. You ain't shit," Grady yells out as I'm walking out.

"Fuck you," I yell back at him. That's all I can say. I'm too upset to say more to him right now.

CHAPTER 10

"I thought about what you said the other day. If I want a bigger cut, I have to give you bigger work. So I got a job for you. If you want it," Grady calmly talks to me over the phone.

"Okay, what do you have for me," he's trying to make amends for once. Maybe I'll follow his lead and we can put as much of this behind us as possible.

"We're trying to expand, and link up with a crew over in Chicago. They've already come here, and showed their faces. Kissed ass and all that. Now we need to do an exchange. Someone has to take the product up there, and it's a lot of product. Has to be someone I trust. I know you don't like me, and I don't like you. But I think you can get it done. You willing to make that trip? It's four hours, almost all highway and going through a bunch of farms. Can you do that?"

"Yeah, I think I can handle that."

"Bring your boys along with this one. If you trust them, they'll be good to have. Nothing wrong with bringing numbers as long as it isn't crazy. Don't take any guns. They're going to check you out when you get there. If you show up with guns, it's going to look crazy. You got any questions."

"When do we need to go?"

"Today. The car is loaded up and ready to go. Product

is in the trunk where the spare tire would go. Just pick it up at the office and hit the road ASAP. I'll text you the phone number for the guys you're meeting."

"Alright, I'll get it done."

"One last thing, don't fuck this up for me," there's the Grady I know.

After he hangs up I put in for an uber to take me to his so-called office. I give Nate and Tevin the rundown of the situation over the phone. Tevin is excited, he's been ready for something bigger for a long time. He's got a one-track mind and drug dealing is the only thing he wants to do. Nate, isn't so sure about it. He's coming, but he's nervous. He's got good reason to be. This is basically the point of no return for us. After this, we don't have any options about career paths. We're solidified in it. Admittedly, Nate managed to make me a little nervous about all of this.

Once we do this, we're really drug dealers. Transporting drugs between states, that's an upgrade from a few pills at some parties and night clubs. We can't really don't have any way to go back from this, at all. His bigger worry is that Grady is not only being nice to us, but trusting us as well. Those are both reasons to be nervous. I hadn't even thought about what made Grady change his mind so much overnight. If the crew from Chicago has already been here, why didn't they take the drugs back with them? Nate is paranoid, but he's usually got a good reason. I just hate that he was so damn convincing. Now it'll be in the back of my mind all day.

Still I take the car and head back to the hotel where I told them to meet me as if everything was fine. I make my way upstairs to my room to grab a change of clothes for the trip. I open the door to my suite and to my surprise Officer Flagg is sitting on my couch enjoying some leftover Chinese food and watching TV as if it were his place. I can't manage to think how he not only tracked me down but got in.

"I've been waiting for you Jason," he turns off the TV

and invites me over to have a seat.

"My name is Javon. You've got my license, you should know that."

"Doesn't do me much good when you abandon your home," he flings my driver's license at me.

"Yeah, I had a pig problem. Had to leave for a minute."

"You've got a smart-ass mouth. Especially for someone I left crying in the street last time we met," he reminds me of our first meeting.

"I didn't cry. I was just pissed."

"Well, I hope you have my money."

"Here, let me check my pockets really quick," I fiddle through all my pockets. "I've got a five dollar bill for you," I laugh.

"Boy, I got half the mind to blow your brains out right now," he stands up and removes the snap from his holster.

"Honestly, the way things are going lately, you might be doing me a favor," I'm only half joking.

"We got a 10-31, any units near," the radio crackles to life.

"You're so lucky, I'll be back. Don't try to run again," he walks out answering his radio.

No sooner than he leaves is there a knock at the door. I look through the peephole just to see Tevin staring back at me. I open the door and they rush in quickly and slam the door behind themselves.

"Why the fuck is there a cop in your room," Tevin yells out forgetting his inside voice.

"Why are you living in a hotel," Nate asks much calmer.

"You snitching nigga," Tevin asks louder than before as he steps closer to me.

"I know Grady hasn't been good to you, but there's other ways to deal with him," Nate tries to console me.

"Can I talk," I ask cutting off Tevin's next question.

"Yeah go ahead," Nate is so patient.

"I'll tell you when the time is right. For now, don't worry about it. Nobody is snitching. Nobody is going to jail. The cop, isn't a factor. I promise," that's all I can do to calm them down.

"I'll take your word for it," I can't tell if Nate is mad, confused or disappointed. Probably all three.

"Whatever, but you got a nice ass hotel here," Tevin says making himself comfortable.

"Well enjoy it while I finish packing."

I make sure to pack everything I'll need to move to a different hotel. I can't go home right now but clearly, he found me. I guess I should just pay for the next hotel in cash. I need to lower my standards. I'll switch to a motel. You can pay in cash there; they don't ask questions and are usually away from the main roads. I'm not sure when I'll tell Nate and Tevin about the cop, or Tiffany, the other cop. Why are all these damn cops coming into my life now? Maybe I just stay in Chicago until I figure this out. I need to get a crooked cop out of my pockets. I need a mostly clean cop to stop asking me to snitch. I need to get out the drug game. I need to figure out what to do with my uncle because I can't just let him terrorize the streets.

"You good," I didn't notice Nate had followed me into the bedroom of the suite.

"Yeah, why do you ask?"

He closes the door "because you're stomping around and mumbling to yourself. You're living in a hotel and getting visits from cops. Something is wrong. You can tell me."

"Nate, I just need you to trust me. When the time is right, I'll tell you everything. For now, let's just go to Chicago."

"Look, I'm not someone who likes to pry, but you're the homie, and you aren't good. I just need to make sure you're right before we go out here and you kill yourself or something. Whatever you're dealing with. I can help."

"Can you two stop playing with yourselves and come

on, we got money to make," Tevin yells from the other side of the door.

"We're coming," Nate yells back.

"I bet you are," Tevin laughs at his own joke.

"I promise you, I'll tell you everything soon."

I give the keys to Nate to get the car ready while I check out of the hotel. I won't be coming back here. I toss my bags in the trunk and take a spot in the back seat of the car. Nate is driving which means we won't get in any trouble. He's the safest driver I know. Won't even pull off until everyone has a seatbelt on, always uses his blinker and never does more than five over the speed limit. We might not make it in time but that shouldn't be a problem. The bigger threat, Tevin is in charge of the music. That means he's about to bang bang, shoot em up kill em us to death until we can change drivers.

CHAPTER 11

"So, who you think is better? Nas or Jay Z," Tevin starts up this conversation for the hundredth time. He knows where it'll go. "For me I think Jay is better. Nas got trash beats, he always talking that pro black stuff and never doing any of it. You heard Jay how you go from black girl lost to you owe me for ice?"

"Tevin, we've already had this argument before," Nate says, keeping an eye on the road.

"I'm just trying to settle it once and for all," Tevin responds.

"You heard Blueprint2," I ask. Planning to put this whole thing in a coffin quick.

"Yeah I heard it. Everyone heard it," Tevin gets defensive.

"Okay, so the whole song is just Jay complaining about how people know Nas is better than him. He even says he lost but it doesn't count because he learned a lesson. Even Jay thinks Nas is better. Let it go, no need to keep defending him. He's a grown rich man. He's top two rappers ever, but he's not one. Let it go," he doesn't know how to respond and we can ride to the music before he finds something else to debate.

"What about Game or 50 Cent," he asks after a few minutes.

"Game," Nate and I respond simultaneously.

"Oh, I guess we all feel the same on that one. Kind of hard to argue when only one is still selling records," Tevin sounds defeated even if we all agree.

"We should all become rappers, then we can stop arguing about who is the best. It's so easy to get famous now. Just have to dye our hair and say some gangster stuff," Nate jokes to change the mood.

"My name is Tevin, I got about ten Mac-11s no 38s shots go through you make you trade straws for plates," Tevin starts to rap as Nate and I laugh. "Can y'all do better," he challenges us.

"Roses are red, and violets are blue, lot of people dead, the families coming for you. Have to call up the crew, but they mad too," Nate starts.

"Just drive and keep those Sugar Hill Gang raps to yourself," Tevin jokes.

"Why you laughing Javon? You don't have any bars," Nate says staring into the rearview mirror.

"Okay I got you," I laugh. "Tevin got the Mac-11 but Javon is a lot like Bond, James Bond, make the ladies fond. Nate got a lot of hate, that's why he can't be great. Look there's some wheat and a lake," I thought I had something.

"Boo," Tevin yells.

"Whatever man, just pick some new music so I don't have to keep killing it whit my bars," I joke.

"You're not killing anything with those bars except for us," Nate responds.

"Pull over at the next exit, we can get some pizza," Tevin suggests.

I'm not against it, who doesn't like pizza? Fair Oaks? I've never heard of this town before. From the looks of it, they probably haven't heard of black people before. Still, everyone loves pizza and cash. Shouldn't be any issues. We take our seats and place our order. A few looks, mostly confusion. I'm guessing a few people have only seen a black person on TV and not in person.

"So, when you gonna tell us about the cop," Tevin asks

as if this is a normal conversation.

"You're not going to let it go are you," I ask.

"I just need to know if you're snitching on us," he asks. Nate stares out the window with no input.

"Please, let it go. I'm not snitching on anyone. I promise, it has nothing to do with anyone else. I'll explain later. But for now, we're good," I try to reason with Tevin which never works.

"Alright, but if I find out you're snitching you know what's happening," is Tevin threatening me? He's made threats before, but this is a real threat. I can feel the intensity in his voice.

"You'll snitch with him. I probably will too. You know we're an inseparable team. Jordan, Pippen and Rodman, except we're all getting paid like Pippen. Seven years, eighteen million, he's crazy," Nate jokes to ease the tension.

"I play for the Tevinville Tevins," Tevin says, still annoyed.

"Tevinville ain't got no hoes and they have shootouts every week. Wouldn't want to play there. Playing there would have everyone looking like Stephen Jackson at Club Rio. Natesburgh is a great place to start a family," Nate just keeps the joke running. He's usually not this social but he's trying to cover for me and he can be funny when he puts his mind to it. He always has my back and one day I need to find a way to repay him for that.

"I've never seen either of you with any hoes. But Javon you're a secretive guy. You probably got a little secret something. Probably a cougar. You like them old right," Tevin pretends he's joking but I can still see he's upset.

We finish the meal with Nate mediating the conversation. I get that Tevin is upset; I'd be upset too if I saw a cop coming out of his place. But he keeps pushing the issue when I told him there's nothing to worry about. He's like a German Shepherd, he never lets go when he has the issue. Sometimes it's better for everyone involved if he just drops the issue entirely. That's why Nate always has to keep us from going at it. He swears he's super thug or something, when that just isn't true.

I drive the rest of the way there with Tevin in the backseat. Still referring to me as a snitch until he falls asleep. Nate isn't far behind. They insisted we finish the whole pizza instead of taking leftovers. Now they're all full and sleepy. The quiet does give me some time to think about everything going on. Maybe I need to just meet Flagg somewhere secluded, put a bullet in his head and call it a day. Just pray nobody links the murder to me. I've never shot anyone before, this has got me thinking of taking extreme measures. Maybe I should just snitch on everyone, including Flagg. I don't know what to do in a situation like this.

"You're mumbling to yourself. You good bro," Nate sits up from his nap and asks me as we enter Chicago.

"Yeah, I'm good," for now I just need to focus on the task at hand.

CHAPTER 12

GPS stops tells us we've arrived at a small pawnshop just inside Chicago. This seems like the kind of place my uncle would love. Looks like a business on the outside and inside. Probably a lot of space to handle business in the back likely a small warehouse of space in the back. I'd be willing to bet they don't have any inventory other than what's on the shelves out front. This is a front if I ever saw one. Good enough to the naked eye but any cop or street-smart person would get suspicious of this place. A pawn shop with no business on a weekday?

Tevin is his usual cheery self. He wants to carry the bags because he thinks it'll make him look important. Nate is his usual panicked self, sweating through his shirt at the moment. I take one of the shirts from my personal bag and have him change into a darker hoodie. Something that won't show the sweat as easily as his current clothes. He's sweating through his shirt and it isn't even sixty outside right now. Doesn't look good to go into a meet nervous. Still, I can't blame him this time. Something about this whole thing just feels wrong now that I'm outside the place. We're out in Chicago to meet with some people we never met who were supposedly just meeting with my uncle a few days ago. At a meeting that I wasn't invited to, despite being at almost every single prior meeting. Javon, you're stupid for not asking more questions.

"Hey, watch out when we go in here. Something feels off," I try to let the guys know to keep a look out.

"Fuck that, we're about to get paid. Your uncle is getting paid so he'll be off our backs we got this," Tevin is bouncing on his toes now.

"Can I stay in the car," Nate asks.

"No, we'll be in and out real quick," a promise I can't keep for sure.

I lead the way into the pawn shop with Tevin in the middle and Nate following up. Inside it looks like it could be a real business, with the exception of all the men armed with guns. They rush us, nobody pulls a gun but we get a rough pat down and they look inside Tevin's bag to see the product.

"You must be Grady's boys, follow me," the smallest in the room leads us to the back.

"We're not Grady's boys. Just him. Grady is his uncle daddy," Tevin jokes.

The goon laughs and we keep walking. I need to punch Tevin in the face as soon as we get out of here. Maybe even leave him in Chicago. We're taken to a storage space behind the actual store. Maybe they are running a real business. It isn't well lit but you can see larger appliances, some televisions and other things to be sold off. There aren't as many guys back here, but still enough to keep me nervous. The odds aren't really in our favor here tonight. If something does go down, we're done for. We finally stop at a table in the back of the warehouse area. Behind it stand two men, dressed in suits. Trying their best to look professional, but the tattoos on their hands and faces let me know that isn't the case. They're putting on a show, probably because Grady told them to. They don't seem like drug dealers to me. Just hired guns if anything. Our escort leaves us and heads back to the front.

"We got the money," one of them says placing a suitcase on the table.

"Show me the money," Tevin keeps joking as if this

isn't serious.

The taller man with dreadlocks obliges. He opens the suitcase and displays almost a full case of money. This is the moment I realize Grady didn't tell me how much money we were supposed to get. I sell small quantities of drugs. I have no idea what the value on this stuff is. Tevin being the expert he is walks our bag to the table for the men to see. He opens the bag and drops several white bricks onto the table. I've never actually seen so many bricks of cocaine before. I've never seen more than one at a time before this. I just have to pretend I'm not shocked. Still, from what I've seen in movies and TV shows, this doesn't seem right. It's not in the tight plastic cubes I should recognize, more like loose ovals. I know TV shows aren't real, but this doesn't look right compared to drug busts on the news.

"You mind if we test it," the shorter man behind the table says.

"Go ahead," Tevin steps back with Nate and I.

The first man takes a pocket knife and cuts into one of the packages. I expect him to sniff the end of the knife or rub a little on his teeth, but apparently TV has taught me nothing. Instead he sets up a line on the table. He does the entire line as if this is normal business. I'm going through a lot of first right now. My dad never had the drugs around me, nor any addicts so this is the first time I've seen someone do a line of cocaine.

"Well," Tevin asks, desperate to lead this meeting.

The second man pulls a second brick and repeats the process. What was that rule about not getting high on your own supply? I see they don't really care about that rule at all.

"This shit is fake, kill them," one of the men yells out.

Nate turns to run but there are men behind us as well. For once Tevin's machismo makes the right call. He rushes at the men behind the table before they can draw their guns. He lifts the table and slams them into the dock wall. I follow his lead, slamming my fist on the big red button to open the gate. As the dock door opens Tevin pushes the men out. By now gunshots are ricocheting through the building. I pick up a gun and start to fire back. I'm not really aiming at anyone but I need them to back off.

As soon as the door opens Nate makes a run for it. Our car is on the other side of the building so he turns around and runs back to the front. I follow along with Tevin, but he stops. He runs back towards the gunfire. Tevin is trying to fight for control of the money with one of the men from earlier. I hear a car start and know Nate is ready to go. I run back to help Tevin. I kick the man he's wrestling with in the face. This gives Tevin enough time to grab the case and run with me.

"You stupid motherfuckers," I hear Tevin yell out.

Looking over he's been shot in the arm. Fuck this was a set up. I should have known it. My uncle wants me gone and he might do it this time around. Still ducking bullets, we jump into the backseat of the car. To his credit Nate hits the gas and leaves the parking lot before the door can close. A few men come out the front of the store firing, slowly realizing what went down out back. I put my hand out the window and fire back the rest of the bullets in the gun I grabbed.

"I'm going to die y'all," Tevin says.

"Where is he shot at Javon," Nate asks, no longer panicked but in control of the situation.

"In the arm," I yell back over Tevin's screaming as we hit the highway.

"Tie up his arm as tight as you can somewhere above the bullet wound," Nate keeps giving orders.

Fight or flight, that's what they called it in school. When a situation goes bad, some people fight and other people take flight. Animals have it too. Tevin chose to stand his ground. Nate chose to run. I didn't know what to do. I've never known what to do. When Tevin chose to fight, I just followed. When Nate chose to run, I followed. Everyone says the two of them follow me, but I'm the one following them. For all the talk I had about Tevin being unpredictable, and Nate being paranoid they both handled the situation better than I did. I froze.

"Where are we going," I ask Nate.

"There's a vet clinic in Gary about thirty minutes from here. They should be closed for the night. We can stitch up Tevin and get him some pain killers," Nate thought about this.

"Okay, sounds good," who am I to question him?

"Javon, I'm sorry. I know called you a snitch. I said Grady was your uncle daddy and a bunch of other mean shit. But you came back for me. You really did," Tevin is tearing up but he hasn't lost that much blood. He probably thinks he's going to die. "Nate, man I'm sorry for all the stuff I said about you. I just like picking on you. Y'all think I can go to heaven," he starts to pray.

"It's not that serious. Just stop talking and save your strength," I try to comfort him. I don't really know how bad it is or how to comfort him.

We pull into the back lot of a building with a big inflatable puppy dog on the roof. I guess this is the vet Nate found. He gets out of the car, takes some money from the suitcase and tells us to wait. Tevin is leaning against me and almost asleep so that won't be hard to do. His arm has nearly stopped bleeding but he's still in pain. He's whimpering every now and then. Outside I watch as Nate waits for the last lights to be turned off. When the door opens a woman steps out but Nate forces himself along with her back into the building. I know Nate isn't crazy, but I get nervous after a few minutes go by. When they exit the building the woman heads to her car and Nate comes to get us.

"We've got the building for the night, bring him in," Nate says.

CHAPTER 13

Inside Nate leads the way to a treatment room with no animals inside. I help Tevin sit down on one of the big metal operating tables while Nate disappears. Nate comes back with a few pill bottles and some water before disappearing again. This time he comes back with alcohol, a needle, thread and some bandages.

"Take these," he hands the pills and water to Tevin.

"This is a lot of pills," Tevin mumbles.

"Because they're for cats. You're a lot of cats," Nate says back. "Javon, hold him down."

"What for," Tevin asks, back to himself almost.

"Because this is going to hurt. We need to clean the wound and sew it up. The pain killers won't kick in right away," Nate says still calm.

I hold Tevin down on the table as he still tries to bargain and tells us all his fears. Needles, catheters and anything medical really, but this is for his own good. Nate pours alcohol all over the wound and Tevin fights me to get free for a moment Nate wipes away any leftover blood from the wound. It's not a big wound but you can see a front and back so the bullet went through his arm. I guess we should be glad it didn't break any bone on the way through. Tevin fights the whole time, but Nate gets some sloppy sewing done on the wounds. After he rubs some kind of cream on them before covering them with bandages. Tevin falls asleep and we leave him back there to rest.

The two of us go wait in the lobby area. The adrenaline has stopped flowing and Nate is back to normal or as normal as you can be after something like the whole mess we just got out of. There's going to be an even bigger mess when we get home. I don't think I can deal with this mess anymore. Every time I think things are going well and cooling down, something comes up and raises the temperature. This thing I call a life is ridiculous. I can't keep bottling it up either. I'm going to crazy if I do. I'd never tell Tevin anything like this. But Nate, he can handle it. I just have to make sure he's fine. We've been through a lot today and he's been an entirely different person. He's driving without seatbelts, escaping shootouts, bribing people and treating gunshot wounds. I don't even know this guy right now.

"Javon," Nate calls out to me laying on a couch across the room.

"Yeah."

"I need you tell me everything."

"About what."

"Everything. We almost died tonight and I need to know you didn't have us walking into a trap," he turns his head to show me he's serious.

"Where do you want to start?"

"Start with the cop and why you're staying at a hotel."

"Remember the first party we went to after you introduced us to AC?"

"Yeah."

"That's when I met the cop."

"Was he at the party?"

"No, he just pulled me over on my way home."

"What for?"

"Being black on a Friday night. What else?"

"So why are you hanging out with him now?"

"It's not that simple. See, he beat me up, pretty bad. Searched the car, and found my cut of the money. He took it. Told me he wanted more. Took my driver's license and everything. That night I went home and emptied out my house. That's why I started staying in a hotel. I've been dodging him. When you showed up, he had just found the hotel that day. We're not friends. He's trying to extort me. I promise," I look Nate right in his eyes hoping he'll believe me.

He sits up and looks back into my face for a minute without saying anything. He puts his head in his hands and just swears under his breath. That's a lot to take in and it's not even half of what I'm planning to tell him tonight. If this was Tevin we'd be fighting already. Nate is just taking things in. He's calculating like that when he needs to be.

"Why the fuck didn't you tell me. I get Tevin, but you could have told me. We would have figured this shit out," he stands up, clearly mad about the whole situation.

"I didn't want you to get involved. He doesn't know you or Tevin. He just knows me. He wouldn't think to bother you."

"But we could have figured it out before it went this far."

"Okay, lets figure it out now."

"What did you have in mind," Nate sits back down.

"We can kill him."

"You can't kill a fucking cop."

"Okay so how about another cop?"

"You going to tell the police, on the police. You've seen the news, nothing will happen. You'll either end up dead or in jail," he says as if I hadn't thought about it.

"I know another cop who can help."

"Okay Officer Swift, who is the lucky cop behind door number two," Nate asks sarcastically.

"Well, there's this woman Tiffany," I start.

"Cop pussy, is that what you like? I've been trying to figure you out for a while now, but wow," Nate interrupts.

"No, she's not like that. She says she knew my dad. She wants me to testify against Grady," I try to explain, this sounds crazier than the last one.

"So, you are snitching," he throws his hands in the air.

"No I'm not snitching. I just met her."

"Do you trust her?"

"I don't know. She seemed legit and hasn't really pressed me or anything. Just said it was option. Told me the street life isn't what my pops wanted and I wasn't built for it."

"Well, based on tonight, neither of us is built for it. If you have to tell, I'll tell with you. I got a little money saved, we can move to the middle of nowhere, but we'll be alive," Nate is serious which brings a quick end to my laughter.

"We could kill Grady," I suggest.

"You'd have to do it. Nobody else can get close to him. He only lets you get that close because of your mom. Even Stack has to go through security to speak with him."

"But he set us up tonight. This had to be all him, nobody else would do something so bold. It just doesn't make any sense if he didn't."

"He probably thinks you're out to take over. You can't reason with someone like him. All the more reason you need to call that lady cop. Let her know you'll snitch. It's not like she has charges against you. Just make her promise immunity or something. That's all we got right now," Nate nearly begs me.

"I guess I don't have a choice here. She might be willing to help me out with Grady. But how do I know she isn't friends with the crooked cop?"

"You just have to trust her. Ask her some questions only people who really knew your dad would know. His favorite ice cream flavor or something like that. Usually you have time to get to know people, but right now we don't have that luxury."

"Alright, I guess I'll set up a meeting with her. You want to come?"

"Hell no," Nate suddenly has plenty of energy to tell me no.

"So for now what do we do?"

"Keep moving around. Don't answer calls from Grady. Keep calls to your family brief and from phone numbers they don't know. In fact, put your phone in airplane mode so they can't call you and track the cell towers or leave it somewhere else."

"Nate, we're dealing with drug dealers and crooked cops. Not the FBI."

"You never know. Just have to be careful. You got us in some deep shit, you know that right?"

"I know, this is the last time, I promise."

"No it isn't. You can't' go a week without getting into some kind of trouble," we both laugh at Nate's joke because it's true.

"You get us in trouble too. Remember when you were trying to sell bootleg CDs in gym class?"

"Okay, I didn't try. I did it. Just not as smooth as I wanted it to be."

I didn't sleep well that night. Tevin seemed to be doing better in the morning. He also agreed that my uncle probably set us up. We thought about staying here for a while but they would come looking. The people in Chicago saw us get on the highway. There's only one way we could go from there. Nobody came looking for us last night, but they probably will this morning. Nate suggested we get a change of clothes at Walmart, grab something to eat and head back home from there. Tevin is still a little out of it from the cat pills but he'll be okay.

I rent a car from the only place in town that will take cash and we head back to the city. Nate doesn't fill Tevin in on what's going on. Still, he can sense that we're in the middle of something crazy. There isn't much talk on the way home. No debates about which artist is better or any freestyling. We all just stare out into the nothingness of the highway for the most part. None of us know what's coming next, but we're all afraid of it.

CHAPTER 14

"Alright, we'll split up here," Nate pulls over about a few blocks from our cars.

"You're just leaving us here," Tevin asks.

"Yes," I get out the car and grab my bag.

"Javon, go straight to your car. Tevin wait here with me. When Javon drives by, go to your car. I'm going to take this rental and disappear," Nate is still in control here.

"Sounds good to me. We can meet up later. Stay safe," I start making the walk towards my car, curious how much Nate will tell Tevin.

I know I should be afraid; my uncle could have people popping out to shoot me at any moment. I'm just hoping he isn't that crazy. Still, I'm comfortable for some reason. Almost as if death is a long sleep I've been waiting on, a sleep where all my dreams will come true. Tevin said it was my uncle's city when we told him we were coming back here. The thing is, this is my city too. I thought I would just come here and say my goodbyes, then leave. But just walking through these streets, I realize I couldn't stay away from here for long. I'd always find my way back sooner or later. I always do. Maybe I need to be proactive with this one. I've always run away from my problems, or left them for someone else to deal with. This time I need to handle it myself.

Nate might have had the right idea. Call Tiffany. She's creepy and knows too much about me and I don't know anything about her. Still, she doesn't seem like a bad person. She didn't give me any bad vibes. Maybe I do need to testify against my uncle. It might be the only way out of this. What do I say to her? Hey, my uncle tried to kill me, let's put him in jail. I don't know. I probably shouldn't call her. I can handle this on my own. I've never actually shot at anyone before last night and I wasn't even shooting to kill, just get away. Now I'm thinking about shooting my uncle in the face. What the fuck am I doing?

I wave to Nate and Tevin as I drive by. Tevin hops out the car and starts walking. I'm going to call Tiffany. If not for me, for Nate and Tevin. Nate is probably the best friend I've ever had. I don't really care for Tevin but he has his moments. They don't have anything to do with this family feud but they got roped in because of me. Tiffany might be the only way all three of us can come out of here in one piece. I'll make the call, even if I hate every second of it. I pull her card from my wallet and dial the number. The phone rings a few times before going to voicemail.

"Hey, you've reached Detective Tiffany Carter, I'm away from my phone at the moment, if you leave a message I'll get back to you ASAP. Crime doesn't sleep and neither do I," was that her way of making a joke?

"Tiffany, this is Javon. You stalked me. We need to talk about my dad, my uncle and you. I'm willing to testify or whatever. I just need your help. Things are getting way out of hand. I'm on my way to a motel right now. I'll text you the address when I get there. If you were serious about helping me, I need you to prove it. Call me," I hang up, no need to listen back to my message. I probably sounded a little desperate.

☐

CHAPTER 15

"Hey, thanks for coming," I invite Nicki into my motel room.

"I have to admit, this isn't as nice as the hotel we met in. I thought you said you were financially secure," she jokes, but jokes are based in truth.

"Yeah, things have been a little crazy lately. Just trying to keep a low profile," I laugh to lighten the mood.

"So you called the prostitute, sure," she lets out and audible laugh.

"Your car didn't say anything about sex. If it did, things might have gone different."

"You were going through a lot then."

"What makes you think I'm not going through a lot now," I take a seat on the edge of the bed.

"I can look at you and tell you're going through a lot. You haven't had a haircut since I saw you last. You're in some run-down motel. Pretty easy to tell you're going through a lot," she sits at the small table near the window.

"How much can you go through before you're someone else entirely," I ask her.

"Oh, you're trying to get deep right away. Well," she thinks. "I suppose, you'll always be you. Depending on how far you go, you might be a new version of you, but you'll still be you."

"You sure about that?"

"What are you thinking?"

"Murder. My uncle I told you about. The one fucking my mother. He set me up."

"Then leave. You're still alive. Pack a bag and go. You told me you didn't like drug dealing anyway. Go off and go to school or something."

"You said you don't like being a... talkstitute. But you're still not running."

"No, but I'm going to graduate this winter and be a therapist. How many prostitutes really talk? That's where I come in, I actually talk to people. They come in looking to pay me for sex, they're just going to be upset. I'm good at it. You need to find what you're good at and do that. Murder isn't the right solution. Why are you two beefing anyway?"

"What do you mean why? He had my dad killed and immediately started shacking up with my mother. How am I supposed to be okay with that? Then he tried to have me killed."

"This sounds like some Shakespeare stuff. Maybe you should speak to your mother. If you find out where you two stand you might feel different."

"We're not really speaking right now."

"Why not," she moves to the bed taking a seat next to me.

"We had an argument. Basically, she wants to be in control of everything. I always just did what she wanted. I didn't really want to, but dad always made me do it. Without him around, I just can't keep doing the stuff she wants."

"Have you told her that?"

"No, haven't tried."

"Why not?"

"I used to try opening up to her when I was younger. She never cared, didn't listen. So I just stopped. I figured the less she knew the better."

"You should call and tell her how you feel."

"Why? So she can just start yelling and not hear anything?"

"Even if she starts to yell, just yell back. Tell her how you feel until she gets the message."

"Sometimes I believe it would be better if she had never birthed me. I'm proud, vengeful and ambitious. I've done more, bad things, than most have thought of. Yet, I have dark thoughts and an ill imagination. What do I do with those? How long before I act on those? I am not a bad person, at least, I don't believe I am."

"Damn. That's a lot. I don't have the answers to all of that. For now, I'd say, do something good. Try to write the wrongs you've done. Make amends. As for that little dark cloud you call a mind you might need anti-depressants or something. I can't help you with that. You might need to see a real doctor."

Who needs a therapist when you've got Nicki? I feel a little better. None of my problems are solved. I didn't really expect her to solve them. I just needed to get some stuff off my chest. Putting all of that her isn't the best way to handle things. She doesn't deserve that, but who else could I tell? Nate knows what's going on but even if he's trying to be calm, cool and collected right now, he's a ball of nerves. He'd break down and start trying to form suicide pacts. Tevin, is Tevin. Stack works for Grady, I can't go to him even if I trust him.

What's that saying? Can't turn a hoe into a housewife? Don't put your tongue on a prostitute because you have to kiss your kids? I don't know. I don't care either. It isn't like she's a real prostitute. I close my eyes and lean in towards Nicki. I wait for her to meet me half way and she never does. I open my eyes and she's just shaking her head at me.

"Javon, I like you. In another life, we'd make a great couple. But right now? I've got a lot going for me, and well you're just too fucked up," she says to me as I pull back.

"Aren't you a prostitute? What if I pay?"

"Nope. I told you, I don't do sex. Besides, I'd consider you a friend now. I don't even sell talks to friends. I'm not even going to charge you for the talking. I just want you to get yourself right."

"Sorry, I shouldn't have pushed it. I just thought since we were…I don't know what I was thinking."

"Don't be sorry. You waited for consent; a lot of men don't do that these days. Like I said, if you weren't going through your own little Greek Tragedy and I wasn't on the verge of my next step in life, we might have worked. You're a good man, don't do something you're going to regret forever. If you think on it, I'm sure you'll find a way out of this," she makes her way to the door.

"Do you want me to at least walk to your car," the only thing I can offer her that she might take.

"Yes, because I don't know if that's a crackhead or a racoon outside but it's big and it's scaring me. I was going to ask you to walk me out anyway but then you wanted to be all kissy," she jokes bringing back the comedy.

I walk Nicki to Nicki to her car and we part ways with a hug, a friend hug. I've never seen myself as someone obsessed with sex. If it comes, it comes. I've never chased after it. Still, Nicki was the first woman to ever reject my advances. Now I'm just thinking about her so much more. Maybe I'm not as good looking as I thought I was. Then again, she's the only woman who didn't know my father, or my friends. She just knows me as Javon. What if Javon just sucks as a person? Am I not likeable? I've told her everything about me because I thought prostitute would make great therapist. Sometimes it sucks to be right. Maybe that's why she doesn't like me, she knows how messed up I am in the head.

She's right too. I need to take some steps to change my life for the better. I'm motived. I try call my mother but the phone goes straight to voicemail. Something tells me it isn't coincidence. One thing about run down motels is they still have payphones. A quick trip to the office to get some quarters and I'm making a call. It rings this time, so she's got my number going straight to voicemail.

"Mom, it's Javon. I'll keep it brief. You've been a shitty mom. You've used me, never supported me or thought about my feelings. I used to cry about it all the time, just made sure nobody ever saw. I'm not going to cry about it anymore, it isn't worth it. I told you my uncle was up to no good. He tried to have us killed. If you're still going to be with him, I can't have anything to do with you for my own safety. Even through all that I still love you, and I don't want anything bad to happen to you. It's up to you where our relationship goes from here. Make your choice. You've got my number. Bye."

CHAPTER 16

"Get dressed and get in the car," Tiffany yells up to the balcony of my motel way too early in the morning.

"What? You don't call or text me back for a week, now you just show up yelling get in the car?"

"Don't make turn on the cherries and berries. You got five minutes," she takes a seat in her unmarked car.

People are starting to look out. This isn't the kind of motel where you want to bring police attention. I do as I'm told. I throw on some jeans, a t-shirt and some sneakers. I want to trust Tiffany but she isn't exactly meeting me half way with this. Still, I don't really have many options. Not unless I'm trying to have a shootout in the middle of street with my uncle. That isn't the route I want to take, I'd be out manned, out gunned and stand no chance. So, I'm going to get in her car. Just in case, I send a text to Nate and let him know what's happening. If something is going to happen to me, at least he'll go to the right people. I mean, he's willing to snitch with me.

I hop in her car quickly and I've never been so thankful for tinted windows before. If she doesn't take me to a parking lot and kill me, I would die from embarrassment, being seen with the police. She pulls out the lot and takes off like she knows where we're heading.

"Where are we going," I ask.

"We're going to see what you've been up to."

"I've been sitting in a motel hiding out after my uncle tried to kill me."

"Join the club," she says pulling around a corner slowly.

"He tried to kill you too?"

"No but look around us."

"What am I looking at?"

"Over there on the corner. That man never missed a day of work, then he got hooked on drugs. That woman by the bus stop, she's got three kids at home. She can't pass a drug test, so now she's out here selling her body," Tiffany points out more people and tells more stories.

"Why are you telling me all this," I can't listen to any more.

"If we're going to work together to take down your uncle, I need to know you're not going to take his place. You need to see how messed up he has this people. If you're just going to go into the family business we're done and I can drop your ass off right here. You see these people? This is why I go to work. You want to sell a little weed; I don't care if you're not selling to kids. But this shit? People talk about crack like it ever left. You just have to shine a light in the right spots."

"I understand. But you need to know, I never wanted any parts of the family business. I might not know what I want to do with my life, but it was never this. I never wanted this at all and I know it's fucked up. If we're going to work together, I've got some terms and conditions too."

"What might those be?"

"You need to be honest with me, all the way. I don't know shit about you, but you expect me to trust you. I need you to stop pretending you know who I am. You knew my dad. You know the kid he told you about. I'm not that kid. Lastly, I need you to stop acting like you're so much better than me. I fucked up, I know it. Everyone fucks up. If you can do those three things. We'll be okay. Do we have a deal," I extend my hand to her.

"Yeah, we've got a deal. Let's go get lunch, partner."
"Partner?"

☐

CHAPTER 17

We walk into the little diner and she points to a booth. She shakes some hands with other people. Mostly old white men and women, two or three people in suits and a single officer in uniform. I've never been to this place before, but it gives me the creeps. I don't see any other black people who aren't working in the back. Looking around the pictures on the wall are all of police officers and military folks, that probably became police officers. Blue lives matter hats sitting on almost every one of the tables and I suddenly realize we're in a cop diner. I thought these things only existed on TV.

"Did you bring me to a copstaurant," I ask as Tiffany sits down.

"Yeah, because we'll be safe here. Nobody will look for you."

"Except Sam Flagg."

"I don't know who that is," of course she doesn't know.

"Sam Flagg is a cop, he wants money from me."

"Why does he want money from you."

"He followed me," I lean in and whisper, "from a drug deal."

"Well shit, we need to deal with him before your uncle. He'll kill the whole case."

"So how do we kill him?"

"We can't kill him," she laughs and smiles as if my thought was ridiculous.

"Why not?"

"Why do you want everyone dead? There's easier ways to handle things," she keeps laughing.

"You folks ready to order, or should I give you a few minutes," the waitress interrupts.

"We'll both have a shepherd's pie with water," Tiffany says and the waiter scurries off.

"What is a shepherd's pie?"

"Don't worry, you'll love it."

"So what about the cop?"

"Easy, I'll get you some information, you put on your scary face and deal with it. Try to keep the violence to a minimum, if you do it right, you can have a valuable ally in the future."

"What?"

"Crooked cops are a dime a dozen, but they have their uses when they can be controlled."

"You sound like a crooked cop right now," I look at her, not sure if I should run or not.

"Oh, I'm super crooked. It just matters where your crook bends," at least she's honest.

"That makes no sense."

"One day you'll get it. I might not extort people, or use excessive force but I don't have time to lock people up for weed, so I might let them slide. I don't have time to chase kids for truancy. It's easier to call someone with a warrant than track them down for me. Like I said, crooked cops are a dime a dozen. We just bend different ways."

The waitress comes back with our food. This shepherd's pie stuff isn't bad. It's mashed potatoes and maybe ground beef, but is that gravy? I don't know but it is good, I think there are peas but I like it. I can't believe I'm putting my life in the hands of a woman who proudly calls herself a crooked cop. I supposed the devil that you know is better than the one you don't. Still, who is proud of their crooked cop status? Maybe that's just some kind of cop joke I'm not comprehending. This really is the best meal I've had in so long. I haven't cooked anything since Flagg ran me out of my own house.

"What's the plan with my uncle I ask," taking a break from the food.

"You're going to make him paranoid. Make him think you're coming for the throne."

"How would that help?"

"He'll get paranoid, he'll start making noise, and raising hell. Eventually he'll do something dumb, and we can arrest him on the link. You testify, boom, pow, surprise. We got him," she's so calm about this that I'm going to let the boom, pow, surprise go.

"Alright, but how do I do that? He tried to have me killed not long ago, in case you forgot."

"You keep doing whatever you were doing before that."

"Selling drugs? No, I'm through with that."

"How about this. Does he have any guys working for him that are still loyal to your dad?"

"He's got a few. Stack is the most loyal. But I think he wants out. He just hasn't figure out a way yet."

"Good, we can use that. Give a call to Stack. Nothing crazy. Let him know he should leave town for a while," she rubs her hands together.

"What will that do?"

"Your uncle will think a turf war is coming soon and start to move."

"Okay, I can do that this evening. I know a couple of other guys who were close to my dad too. I'll call them too.

"Finally, we can put that bastard under the jail."

"Why do you want my uncle so bad?"

She doesn't answer right away, "a promotion. I can be the captain of my own squad," I don't believe her. There's something more, but she's not letting it slip. She's keeping her cocky demeanor.

We finish dinner, and she drops me off. For the first time, I don't feel like she's some crazy lady forcing her way into my house. I still don't know anything about her, but I feel like I can trust her. I send Nate a text and let him know what went down. For now, I'll wait. If she comes back to me with the information about the Sam Flagg, I'll know we're going to move on this. What I'll do with the information, I don't know. She took murder off the table, so I can't expect her to help me hide a body. I guess I'll have to get creative with this one, and torture isn't something I'm into. I guess I'll have to dip my toe in the water.

◻

CHAPTER 18

Tiffany came through in the end, I didn't know if she would. She got me a list of all the fuck ups that aren't on Flagg's record. She got me his family addresses. I declined those. I think she was testing me, to see how far I would go. I thought about it for a long time. I realized she was right, and Nicki was right. I'm not a killer. Sometimes I have dreams where I'm just this monster doing anything I want to people, but I'm not that. I could have never killed Flagg, but I am a talker. That's who I am. I can talk myself out of most things. Especially if I have leverage. Now, I've got more leverage than I could ever need on Flagg. Tiffany said he would make a good ally in the future. I don't want to be associated with someone like him. I just want him to leave me the fuck alone.

I pull my truck to the back of his house, no fence or anything separating the alley from his yard. If you can it a yard, there's nothing but dirt and gravel here. I can imagine he would have an alarm. I slide on a pair of thick rubber gloves I picked up from the hardware store on my way over. I approach his power meter and cut the plastic security bracket. Opening the box, I look for a fuse, and pull one, I look at his home and don't see any change. I make my way towards the backdoor and the motion lights don't trigger. Okay, that was easier than I thought. Movies make it look so hard, turns out every firefighter and police officer in the city knows how to do it. I use my small crowbar to pry open his back door and push my way inside.

The whole place smells like urine and beer. Dirty clothes are tossed around the floor, he's got leather furniture with butt prints embedded into them. I figured a dirty cop would live dirty, but this is ridiculous. Dirty dishes float across brown water in the sink. If I had known he was living like this I would have given him the money. He could have got a cleaner, maybe even some slightly less used furniture. I've never seen a house so dirty, that didn't belong to one of those crazy hoarders on TV. I wanted to get comfortable before he finished his shift. Just in case he decided to have a couple drinks after work. I could never get comfortable in this roach infested fire hazard he calls home. I can't wait to strip off my clothes and burn them all.

I can't take the smell for long, so I step out and wait for his car to pull into the driveway. He went out for drinks for sure, either that or he's taking his time getting here. I wouldn't rush to get back to this place either. I hear a car pulling up out front and make my way back inside in enough time to see the headlights turn off. I slip behind the front door and wait for the key to turn the lock. The deadbolt drops in place and the door opens. Muscle memory has him reach for the alarm to key in the code before realizing that the alarm didn't sound when he opened the door.

I slam a brick across the back of his head. He falls to the floor with a thud, never expecting it. He won't stay down for long. I take his gun and drag him to the kitchen. I use his own handcuffs and take his belt. I force myself to take a seat for dramatic effect and my skin starts to crawl. This dude is nasty, Tevin has roaches but at least he doesn't throw a welcoming party for them. I bet Flagg has rats too, you don't even see rats in this part of the country. Stretching his belt out in front of me, I feel like one of those old cartoon villains. I should be saying I've got you now Supernova, you fell right into my trap. Something silly like that.

"What the fuck," Officer Flagg mumbles to himself as he comes too.

"Good morning, allow me to reintroduce myself," I joke, he immediately reaches for his gun. "My name is Swift, Javon Swift."

"What is this?"

"I'm going to kill you."

"You can't kill a cop."

"Says who," I laugh knowing he's right.

"Every cop in the city will be looking for you."

"Sam, I've been thinking a lot. The world is fucked up. I've got family members that want me dead. My mother won't talk to me. I've got a dirty cop, figuratively and literally, trying to extort money from me. Because I got to thinking, you wouldn't know me. You knew my father, and thought to look for me based on my license plates. There was no reason for you to stop me otherwise. You had a plan to see if I took over. I forgive you," he looks away realizing I pieced it together. "Still, some pour soul has it way worse than I."

"Spare me the fairy tales and get it over with," Flagg antagonizes me.

"You know, I actually wanted to be a cop when I was a kid. I never wanted to sell drugs. That's why I kept a low profile. You happened to luck out and actually find me, with drug money at that. You should have left it alone. But you pressed your luck, kept stalking me. Now I've had to decide your fate."

"Fuck you," he spits on the floor.

"Don't feel bad. Other people have decided my fate my entire life. I've never been sure if I believed in destiny. Didn't think I had one. Now, I've got this hunger, this aggression. I want things. I think I'm in love for the first time. There's this woman I like, and I would do anything to have her in my world. She said I need to get my life together first. You're a problem in my life. The first on a long list of problems to solve. I've never killed anyone, I'm not a killer. Just don't have it in me. But now I have to kill you. That presents me with a dilema."

I make my way over towards him and he bucks at me. Cuffed to a fridge, I remember when he beat me. With everything going on, I had actually forgot about it, until I laid eyes on him. I punch him right in the face, then another, and another. I work the body with some punches. I make sure to strike the knees a little. It felt good to get that rage out. Not just for him, but for my uncle and for this dirty ass house. I had a lot of rage.

"Stop, just shoot me, already" he groans.

I might have gotten carried away. I make my way to the stove, and turn on the gas but don't light the burners. The house starts to fill with gas. Toss a fork in the microwave and set the timer for 10 minutes. I pat him on the head as he begs while I make my way out the back door. I just wait as he screams. At seven minutes, I walk back into the house. I turn off the burners and stop the microwave. He's crying and praying, apologizing to god. All while sitting in a puddle of his own tears, sweat and piss.

"Sam, this isn't a movie, I wouldn't be so dramatic if it was. I'm not going to kill you. Now you know I'm not to be fucked with. You can even keep the money you took from me. I just need you to understand this, I don't sell drugs. You don't know me. I know where you live. I know all the laws you broke. I know you steal from evidence. I know where your mother lives. I know your daughter lives with your ex-wife. Sam, if you see me. Cross the street. I don't give a damn if you're in church. If you see me, move around. If you ever cross me again, I will kill you. You've been given a second chance. Don't fuck it up. Do you understand me."

"Yes," he moans.

"Sam, do you understand me. Look me in my eyes."

"Yes," his swollen crying eyes make contact with me.

"Great," I unlock the handcuffs but don't give him his gun back. "I'm going to hold on to these. Don't want you shooting me in the back," I empty the bullets from his magazine and fling them all in separate directions.

Sam doesn't move. He's just glad to be alive. I make my way out the house, I walk backwards with my own gun drawn. If Sam makes a move, I'll shoot him this time. He doesn't follow, and I'm able to get in my car and drive off. At the end of the alley I feel my knuckles. Wet with some of Sam's blood, but still mine. I'm beating up cops now. This is everything my dad didn't want for me. What the fuck am I doing?

I pull down the visor and look in the mirror. This is me, the same Javon I've seen every day in the mirror. Is it? I never thought I could do something like that. I've been doing a lot that I've never done before. All of this shit has been crazy lately. I need to go home. I need to be me. I need to get back to me. But maybe I've gone so far that I'm someone else now.

I'm not going to find myself dipping in and out of hotels. My uncle doesn't know where I live anyway. I don't know what I would do if he showed up. I'm someone completely different now. I'm working with police. I'm possibly in love, I'm beating people within an inch of their life. I had a fucking shoot out, things have been so crazy I forgot that. I need to end all this. If I keep going, I'm going to keep doing more and more things until I cross a line I can't come back from and I don't even know where that line is for me. I need to end this as soon as possible.

My uncle wants me, he can come get me. I'm done with the hiding. Tiffany wants me to make it look like an uprising is coming. I'll give her more turmoil than she can handle. I can't keep waiting. I slam on the gas and peel out of the alley, music blaring, not caring. I've got empires to watch crumble.

CHAPTER 19

"Last night there was another shooting. This time outside of the strip club. This shooting is believed to be related to the string of six shootings earlier this week. Fortunately, have been no casualties. This has been your update, stay tuned for the most nonstop Hip Hop and R&B," I switch from the radio to Bluetooth.

My uncle really has been tearing up the streets looking for me. I haven't even done anything crazy. I've stayed quiet and haven't moved around much, tried to stay of sight. The real reason is I've been calling people who were close to pops and telling them to get out of town. Well, not everyone, that would be too suspicious. Just the ones I like. Stack is the only one who didn't resist. Said he'd like to take his wife on a trip this year for Christmas since the kids are out of the house. Anyone I don't like, I didn't give them a call. It would look funny if people I didn't like were getting calls.

So far, he hasn't killed anyone, which is good. It means he actually does have some restraint. Tiffany called it. I thought he would shoot up every house, business, trap, and club he knew his people went too. She knew him better than I did, maybe she did grow up with him and pops. I keep meaning to ask her about that. I'll probably ask her today. Either way, if he doesn't get answers soon things are going to get worse. He'll start killing people eventually. So far, the cops haven't linked any of the shootings directly back to him, but it's only a matter of time.

Whatever plan Tiffany came up with has to be working, but it's working too slow. I need to know when we're moving on to the next step. A couple of people I don't know or don't like getting shot, doesn't mean anything to me. I know that's wrong but, eventually it'll get worse. Someone innocent will catch a bullet sooner or later. Hell, for all I know someone could have got a stray already. Six shootings have been reported, but for all I know he could have dropped a couple bodies in the White River, that's out of style, but it was what all the killers were doing back when I was young. He's a man of habit.

I'm thinking about this too much. I walk into the restaurant that Tiffany brought me to and take a seat. This time I order beef stroganoff, the food here is so good. I never heard of half of it. I order the veal for Tiffany. Haven't had a bad meal here yet. If there weren't so many cops, I'd here all the time. I'm surprised Tiffany didn't beat me to the spot, she usually does by half an hour if I believe her. I really stand out in here, there's all kinds of races, genders and age groups, but all these cops dress alike. They tuck anything into their pants, polos, button downs, t-shirts; I wouldn't be surprised if someone tucked in a winter jacket. Who teaches cops this? They don't have a class on dress codes at the academy? This is why undercover cops are easy to spot. They still dress like cops when undercover.

"What's so funny," Tiffany asks walking in as I chuckle to myself.

"Cops."

"What about cops?"

"Do y'all tuck in everything? Shirts, hoodies, coats, what is that," I try to hide my smile.

She pauses and giggles, "I couldn't even tell you if I wanted to. I've been wondering the same thing since the academy. People just come in like that, for no reason," we laugh as the food arrives.

"I ordered for you, I remember you said you loved the lamb."

"I do, but lamb is expensive."

"This one is on me, if you tell me what I want to know?"

"Okay, shoot," she says with a mouth full of food.

"Pops told you a lot about me, but he never mentioned you. How did y'all meet?"

"Oh, that's easy. We were neighbors, grew up three houses down. Went to the same school and everything. We were inseparable as kids. All the way through high school."

"What happened then?"

"Well, it's complicated. I guess, we grew apart and I became a cop," she pauses and looks out the window.

"I feel like there's more you're not telling me."

"Maybe," she turns back to her food.

"You dated him, didn't you? I could see him with someone like you. Bad jokes, not afraid to be in control, but not demanding. I bet y'all were cute," I laugh.

"You sure you want to go down that road?"

"Yeah, what happened?"

"We had an argument. Something stupid, I can't even remember now. But, we took a break. During that break, he got another woman pregnant," she sniffs a big breath of air through her nose. I'm not sure if she's trying to stop tears or just annoyed thinking about it.

"My mother," I still push for more. I don't know why. I move my food around the plate just to listen.

"Yeah it was her. I don't think he even loved her. But, he got her pregnant. Said even if the condom did break, he had to do the right thing. He married her. We just fell apart after that," I don't respond. I'm a broken condom baby. How do I respond? "I changed my major to criminology and then I became a cop. Part of me wanted to get back at him. I knew what he was doing and I wanted to put him behind bars. That was…just so…petty of me.

When I had the chance, I didn't. I realized I was mad at him for doing the right thing. He would call, and I would ignore it. Sometimes I wonder why I didn't answer sooner. I think I was still mad and didn't want to make time."

"You had your own thing going on. You can't blame yourself for that."

"I know that, but it still hurts. It used to hurt more, but then we came back together by accident."

"Were you…a…" I can't get the question out.

"No, I wasn't a side piece. Let that go. I'm too classy to be a sideline hoe and he had too much respect for me. I had too much respect for his sham of a marriage, no offense. I wasn't going to be the one to tear it up. Even if I did want it gone, he wanted it gone. Your mom was the only one who loved the whole marriage thing. Made her feel important. Again, no offense but it doesn't look like you're taking any. We just happened to run into each other one day and started catching. Did you ever wonder why your dad didn't have the turf wars your uncle does?"

"Not really, I just thought I was kept away from that."

"No. See something, say something."

"You saying he was a snitch?"

"No, but when rivals were getting violent, doing something out of line. He might have someone call and leave a tip. Kept his rivals in line, helped us put a way a lot of dealers. It's like I said,"

"All cops are crooked," I finish the sentence for her.

"Got it, but you didn't bring me here for that did you," she changes the subject.

"No, but I had to know. The streets, they're getting wild. Six shootings, probably some beat down that didn't get reported. When are we going to move?"

"Honestly, I don't know. I'm having a hard time getting my superiors to listen to me. Once I get them on board I can move forward with some warrants and we can start picking up people. Did you get the ones you wanted to save out of town?"

"Most of them, a few wanted to stay, but the older guys took vacations."

"Good. You think about what you're going to do when this is over?"

"Take a vacation, don't sell drugs, after that, I don't know."

"You'll need a career."

"Please don't say it."

"Be a cop Javon."

"I knew you were going to bring that back up."

"I'm just saying, your dad always talked about it."

"Do you have kids? Can I tell them to be cops?"

"I have a son, that's it. He already wants to be a cop, but he has asthma and glasses, he won't make it," she jokes.

"Have some faith in the boy," I laugh.

"What about you? How's the family? Any special friends I should know about?"

"Just a mom that hates me. I have a lady I want to be special. She doesn't want me until I get my life together. Real job and all that."

"Cop is a real job."

"I don't like cops."

"You're eating dinner, in a cop diner, with a cop, talking about locking someone up. Boy, you are a cop," she laughs but I can only shake my head at the absurdity of this all.

"How can I be a cop?"

"What do you mean?"

"You worked with a drug dealer, to arrest more drug dealers. But I handcuffed a cop to his fridge and beat him until my hands hurt and you didn't even ask about it. I've sold drugs, a lot. I'm a college drop out. I come from a family of criminals. I'm not like you. I can't walk in that world like you. I'd be a fraud."

"So? Have you seen how many police officers kill innocent people, sometimes kids? Then they go back to work? Cops are fucked up. We do a job that needs to be done. But too many bad cops slide through the cracks. We need more police that will make a change and not bring their bullshit to the job. You've got a lot of bullshit, but you're not going to sell drugs anymore. You can't bring a fridge to work. A college degree isn't required and you probably can't fight anyway. Think about. You did some bad things, but you can tell right from wrong and you don't take advantage of people that trust you, or use people. You can do this. Just think about it."

"I already have," I turn from Tiffany to the waitress walking by "could you bring the check."

"Nah, you're paying so I want some cheesecake," Tiffany says and the waitress nods.

☐

CHAPTER 20

The News has been pretty quiet lately. Streets have been quiet too. My uncle is calming down, maybe he realizes I was just leading him on. Tiffany may have waited too long to get the warrants. I'm pretty sure he's still looking for me. He knows I'm not dead and he isn't a man that stops until he has what he wants. If there's anything I admire about him, it's the tenacity he approaches life with. Like a German Shepherd that gets a taste of blood. Meanwhile, mom hasn't called. I get the feeling she just doesn't care. She'll care about whichever one of us leaves this thing alive, or not in a cell. Admittedly, it's kind of disappointing that she hasn't tried to reach out to me after all this time.

Tires screech outside the house and I hear a car door slamming, with people yelling. This is it, he found me. I knew I shouldn't have come back home. It wasn't worth the risk. But, I was sure he wouldn't be able to find me. I grab my gun and take cover behind the couch. It won't be much protection but I can get the jump on whoever steps through the door. Doesn't matter if they come through the front of the back. I place my finger on the trigger and aim at the door but nothing ever comes through either side.

I peak outside and see a body lying on my front lawn. I can't make out who it is in the dark, but they aren't moving. Thousands of possibilities rush through my mind.

It could be a trap. My uncle could be framing me for murder. I wait for close to twenty minutes before I make any moves or take my finger off the trigger. If someone was coming to kill me. They would have gotten impatient by now, but this body hadn't move. I hit my porch light. I rush out the front door and scan the area with my gun before making my way to the body. I panic when I realize who it is. I'm not even sure how they got him.

"You're okay. You're still with me."

"orry," he tries to say sorry.

"Let's get you in the house."

Fireman's carry, I learned it in gym class. Can carry anyone, no matter their weight. I never thought it would be useful, but here I am. I get him inside the house and drop him down on the couch. He's been beaten pretty bad. Eyes are swollen almost closed completely, both his nose and lips are still bleeding so this is fresh. There're footprints all over his clothes, so they jumped him and stomped him out for sure, this is too much for one person to have done alone. An envelope is actually stapled to his arm, who the fuck has a stapler just laying around? What kind of asshole does something like that? I head to the kitchen and fill a big sandwich bag with some ice. I grab a few towels and some bottled water. Back in the living room Nate is trying not to cry or maybe he's trying to cry and the wounds won't let him. Either way, I know I'd be crying if I were in his shoes. They did a lot of damage. Always trying to be strong for everyone else, like I don't know he's a big crybaby.

I use the water and towels to wipe away the blood, he isn't as bad as he looks which is good. I wrap the sandwich bag full of ice in another towel and place it over his eyes. More important that he can see than talk. I don't really need him to tell me what happened, or apologize. I've got a good idea about what happened already. I take the knife to his arm and pop out the staple as easy as I can. The bloody envelope drops to the floor. He winces in pain but tries not to make a sound. I toss the envelope on the table for now and head to the bathroom. I search for pain killers but I don't have anything stronger than aspirin and they've been expired for a year now. It'll have to do, that's all I've got.

I give him a couple and pour some water in his mouth to help wash them down. I just shake my head at the whole situation, the whole thing is just ridiculous. I'm not mad at Nate. I know he had to tell them where I lived. They probably threatened his life. I would have told too. The Black Terror and Phoen-X was this cartoon I used to watch on Saturday mornings. Super heroes making the world better, taking out the bad guys, giant snakes and all that. Black Terror was bulletproof and Phoen-X could shoot flames of hiss hands. I can't do any of that. I'm not a super hero or anything like that. I'm just a man, the same as Nate is. The same as my uncle. I know he's behind this and I'm done waiting on Tiffany. I've got to handle him as soon as possible. The way men handle things.

"Yo Tevin, you good bro," I ask Tevin as soon as he picks up.

"Yeah, I'm good. You sound messed up tho," he jokes.

"Someone beat the fuck out of Nate and dropped him on my front lawn. I think it was my uncle, so you need to get somewhere safe."

"You sure you don't want an extra gun on this? Since you sound like you're about to get violent."

"Nah, I'm not going to let it come to that. You get somewhere safe."

"Will do, but is Nate good," he asks seemingly concerned for sure.

"Yeah, a little shaken but he's fine."

"Good, don't let anything happen to him."

"I won't, be safe."

"Right," Tevin hangs up.

He's usually more talkative than this but given the current situation, I don't feel like talking either. I grab the envelope from the table and take a seat in the armchair nearest the couch. I rip it open and a picture falls out. A family photo, mom, dad, and I. I've got a few copies of the same photo. This one has a heart around my mother's face. But both my face and my dad's have been crossed out I know it's from my uncle for sure now. He's trying to lure me into doing something stupid. But he doesn't have to, I've already decided I'm going to take care of him tonight. I toss the picture aside and unfold the paper inside. Large handwritten letters fill half the page. Then pen pressed so hard into the page I can feel every word on the back of the page.

Javon you stepping out of line boy. There's no such thing as two kings. If you had stayed in a child's place we would have been fine. You forgot where you came from. You ain't my boy but I raised your dad. You sold my drugs and couldn't bring me my money. You think you're above this organization. My supply wasn't good enough you went and got your own. You telling people get out of this town like you could take me off this throne. I dare you to try boy. I will kill you and every single person you love if you keep fucking with me. You'll end up joining your daddy sooner than later. You got three options. 1. Fall in line and apologize. 2. Leave and never come back. 3. Die. You're gonna stop trying me. I'm done playing games with you. I should have killed you a long time ago.

Should have killed me a long time a long time ago. I agree with that. One of us won't live through this week. This ends now. I make my way upstairs and head into my closet. I bought a bulletproof vest a while back. I was worried someone would try to kill me. Turns out he'll only try to go for the people close to me. Well tonight, I'm walking into the lion's den so I better be prepared. I wish I had a lot more guns to take with me, but I never felt the need. Instead, I just take extra bullets and magazines with me. A pocket knife in case someone gets too close. Hopefully, I won't be in a shootout because it'll be over for me after that.

"Noooo," Nate moans from the coach.

"Sorry, gotta do it."

"My fault. Told them were you leave," his sentence comes out almost right through the swollen face.

"Don't worry about that Nate. Just try to get some sleep alright."

"No, kill you," he tries to get off the couch. I just hold him down with one hand.

"Hey, this has got to stop. You're the first and you're the last to be hurt."

"Noo,"

"Sorry, I got too much love for you fam. I can't let this stand. You would do the same if I was in your position. Just rest. I'll be back."

Nate tries to yell, I just close the door and lock it behind me. I'm not sure if I'll ever come back home, but this needs to be done. I'd rather have him kill me than someone I actually care about. Just have to do things you don't want to sometimes. Either I'm going to the cemetery or going to jail for a long time. Doesn't matter to me anymore. I don't care about the consequences, sometimes I care, but today I don't care. That's who I've always been. I just need to leave all of this in the past so I can move on for better or for worse, because this shit just ain't working.

CHAPTER 21

I park behind my uncle's fake office. I know he doesn't have a security system; no drug dealer does. No regular drug dealer anyway. You don't want the police to respond first, find a bunch of drugs. That would be bad for obvious reasons. You also don't want your nephew prying open your back door with a crowbar but you have to choose one or the other. If your nephew breaks in, well you've brought it on yourself. There's really no way to recover from that because your nephew is going to fuck your shit all the way up.

I make sure my gloves are tighter than OJ Simpson's, then I go to work in the building. Any drugs I find, I bring right to the front. Even if he kills me, when the cops show, there'll be drugs everywhere. He could get away with self-defense for my murder if it comes to that, but he can't run from the drug charges. What? I broke in and sprinkled coke and weed everywhere? Nobody does that. Since the last time I've been here he hung a large picture of himself alongside my mother in the lobby. I fling staplers and tape dispensers at it until it crashes to the ground. Fuck him, and fuck her too for letting him get away with the shit. I get a running start and fling myself into a cubical wall. I feel it snap as I hit the ground the others start to topple like pyramids. I make my way to his office and take a seat in his chair. I dial his phone number.

"Hey, it's Javon. Bring your sloppy Deebo looking ass to work," I leave a message.

I haven't found many drugs yet, but I know they're somewhere in here. He's too cocky to keep it anywhere else. The supply closet is locked which means that's exactly where I want to go. Well, my handy dandy crow bar can handle that. The door doesn't give way easily, but after a little pushing, and ramming I get in. I hit the light switch. Bingo, here's the jackpot. I can leave a trail of bricks right from the front door. This is great, there's some money here too. I guess he didn't follow any of the 10 crack commandments except not getting high. But for all I know he probably does get high. Rules number 7 and 8 are going to be the ones that kill him anyway.

I see he keeps plenty of money here too. He won't miss it. I load it into the back of my truck. If I get out of here alive, I should be paid for all the bullshit I've been through. It doesn't hurt to add it to stockpile. Might come in handy.

"Hey, it's Javon. I know you got my last message you slow, short fat Tiny Lister looking ass motherfucker," message two.

"Hey, I forgot to tell you. You got bigger titties than Destiny's Child. Not just Kelly, Beyoncé and Michelle either. Like, all six of them," message three.

I spin around in the chair. I've really made a mess of this office. I hear a car pull up outside and the door slams. The little bell rings as someone comes through the front door. I pull my gun and aim for the door. I should blow his head off the moment he steps into my view. He walks in gun already drawn but keeping it at his waist.

"Drop the gun," I warn him.

"You drop yours motherfucka," he shouts back.

Fuck it. I fire off a shot. Not to hit him, just to scare him. For someone who swears he's super thug he was afraid. He thought I was going to kill him right there, I thought I might just do it for a moment. He gets the message, and drops his gun. A gaudy, chromed pistol. What purpose does the chrome serve? Did he have to pay extra for that?

"Take a seat," I point the gun towards the chair on the other side of the desk. He sits knowing I'm in charge, "I've got some questions."

"You should have shot me when I walked in. You always have to ask questions, and that's going to be your downfall. You should have shot me, I know you wanted to. Trust your heart."

"Don't give me advice."

"Whatever, if you had took my advice we wouldn't be here anyway."

"We wouldn't be here if you hadn't tried to get me killed in Chicago."

"Oh, you mad about that? Just a little test. You got my money or my drugs by the way," still arrogant with a gun in his face.

"I got a lot of your money. Chicago money and office money. Think I might give it to charity. Do something good with it for once."

"I'll need that back."

"I'll see what I can do about it that. Depends how you answer my questions."

"Hurry up with it. We both know what you want to ask," he's getting belligerent.

"You kill my dad?"

"Yeah, you just now figuring it out? Pulled the trigger myself. Rolled up real slow. You know the rest," he smiles.

"Nah, I figured it out a long time ago. Nobody had anything to gain but you. Just couldn't get anyone to believe me. Story of my life."

"That's because you think you're smarter than everyone else you uppity fucker."

"Next question, why?"

"Because he took what was mine," he grits his teeth.

"What might that be?"

"Everything. The little brother running the organization? How? He took the woman I wanted. Then he didn't do anything with any of it. Didn't expand the turf, only had one kid. Didn't spend any of the money. Just stupid."

"Pops always said your ambition would get you killed now here we are. All because you both liked my mom?"

"He never loved her. I guess you didn't know. He got her pregnant because the condom broke. She was fucking for a rock. She used to be my girl before she got hooked. You're a fucking crack baby. Then he goes and marries her, talking about doing the right thing. Like his name was Mookie or some shit. He should have stayed with the goody two shoes bitch he was stuck on. Could never shut the fuck up about her. What was her name? Tiarra, Tiffany, Tiana, something like that. He had enough, but always wanted mine. You know, I started selling before him?"

"I don't care. Tat's all I wanted to know."

"Oh, you don't want to hear about how your pops was fucking up the game with his morals? He was a snitch. Did you know that? He used to have friends call the cops and tell on other dealers if he didn't like how they were operating or what they did in free time."

"Don't care, just want you dead."

"Take your revenge. Won't change anything. You'll still be a miserable spoiled little brat."

"Yeah, I'll be miserable forever. Made peace with that a long time ago."

"Glad you know it."

"Any last words," I'm stalling. I've been trying to pull the trigger for five minutes now.

"Yeah, more money means more problems. Keep the OGs happy, they'll keep you in charge. Pick one young guy nobody knows about. Make him your replacement."

I still can't pull trigger. I'm hearing tires screech outside and multiple doors slam. Glass shatters outside. I panic.

He smiles, he planned this. He set me up. I knew I should have shot his ass when he walked through that door. I still can't pull the damn trigger. I don't know why I thought I could kill someone. This isn't for me. The gun isn't even pointed at me and now my life is flashing before my eyes because I know how this ends. There was so much I wanted to do, places I wanted to go. Shit.

□

CHAPTER 22

I can't get a plan together before the gun is smacked from my hands. I'm in a fight now. I try to flip the desk over on him. It doesn't work like the movies and he's stronger than I expect. He pushes it to the side with ease. Before I can react, I feel a fist covered in rings go across my face. I need to react, he's bigger than me. I can't out muscle him so I move out of the way. Stick and move, hope he doesn't catch me.

I land a few punches and they don't phase him. He's making his way back around to his gun. I hadn't noticed with all the commotion outside, sirens have been added to the noise. I dive for one of the guns but he grabs me before I can secure it. I'm lifted off the ground and tossed on my back. I still manage to smack the gun under a shelf. He just shakes his head and makes his way to the gun he brought with him. I can't let him get to it.

I dive at the back of his knee. He doesn't fall so I go for the other knee. He's low enough that I can put a chokehold on him. I've got height on my side so it gives me an advantage. The commotion outside is getting louder. I'm not sure what's going on. There's a lot of shouting. I can't worry about that. Just need to choke him out. I know I've got it locked in but he's not fading.

He stands up and flips me over his back. I land on my back and I'm out of breath again. Gasping for breath on my back. He's not moving as fast either. Trying to catch his breath as well. Fuck. I can shoot his ass. I have to. I can't beat him in a fight. If I get out of this, I'll take a boxing class. I start to inch towards the gun. For a third time the air is forced from my body as he kicks me in the gut. He hits harder than I expected, and I expected him to hit hard.

I rush to fight again and feel my shoulder start to burn all the way through. Then I hear the gunshot. Did the bullet hit me before I heard the sound? I glance at my arm, oh shit. I'm really shot. This asshole shot me. I didn't think he was going to do it for real. Fuck, this is it.

"You stupid son of bitch," he walks towards me.

"Fuck you," I say back to him. I want to cry from the pain but I won't give him that pleasure.

"If you beg, I might let you live. I'm not trying to hear your mother's mouth."

"Fuck you. I'll never ask you for anything."

This isn't my proudest moment but I want to live. I want to live so bad. I thought I didn't care about living or dying. But I do, facing down the barrel of gun changes things. Life sucks but I want I to keep living. Now I have to do something I never thought I would. I'm not above begging and that's all he wants. I just won't beg him, never him. I lift my leg with all the strength I've got and kick him right in nuts. It's the only move I've got. He fires off a shot and I duck for cover. I don't know what it hit, but it wasn't near me. I smack the gun but he doesn't drop it. He's somewhere between rage and pain. I try to slither away but he puts one of his feet on my chest and sticks in my place. I can't say I didn't try.

"Drop the gun," I hear someone yell from the doorway. I can't really recognize it.

"Bitch, shut the fuck up," my uncle yells back.

Then I hear a gunshot and he yells out in pain. He drops the gun and I fling it across the room as he struggles with my guardian angel. A few other footsteps rush in the room but I don't have the energy to lift my head and look. He keeps screaming but he's being dragged out of the room.

"Got a pretty little wound there," I recognize Tiffany's voice. I turn my head to see her sitting on the floor next to me.

"I have never been so glad to see your face. How did you find me?"

"One of your friends called me from your phone. He was mumbling. I couldn't really understand what he was saying. I drove over to your house and saw the lights on. Some beat up guy limped to the door and tried to explain what was going on. Eventually, I just had him type it on the phone."

"That was Nate," I interrupt.

"Well, he's a good friend. I didn't get the warrants. This was a probable cause thing. Said I had a tip from an anonymous source that a hostage was held here. So, he's going to be that source in court," she laughs, but he did say he would testify if necessary. "We rushed over. I guess you're the one who left the trail of drugs? Thanks. Saved us some time tearing the place up. But why did you rush over here?"

"He had Nate beat up. Sent me a letter saying he'd hurt everyone I care about. I couldn't let him keep doing it."

"Don't be a dumb ass. Take backup next time, let people know where you're going. You're lucky I knew about this place."

"Won't be a next time."

"Will be when you're a police officer," she laughs.

"Tiffany, I'm bleeding out, maybe dying. Is this a time for jokes?"

"It's not bad. Medics are on the way now."

"Are you lying to make me feel better? It's kind of cold and in the movies, you always get cold before you die."

"It's 32 degrees outside. You rushed over here with a bulletproof vest like it was a winter coat. You dumb ass."

"Thanks Tiffany."

Tiffany stays with me until the medics get here. They put me on the stretcher and wheel me out. This is the first time I've gotten a look at my handiwork in the office. I really made a mess of this place. I owe Nate and Tiffany a big thank you. Without them, I would have died tonight. I need a long vacation after all of this. I can use it to give some thought to my future, because I can't keep doing this street stuff anymore. Andrea was right, this isn't me. I need to go back to college or something. Outside it's snowing and a crowd has gathered. News trucks and people from around the neighborhood.

Tiffany is giving an interview to the news, I guess her promotion is coming soon. I just have to testify. At the end of the day, I'm done with all this. I wanted him dead, but Grady is out of my life anyway. Even if they can't link him to any of the shootings. They caught him with more drugs than needed and I guess my kidnapping. He'll be getting a long sentence as long as the jury doesn't get paid off. Once they shut the doors on this ambulance, it's over.

□

CHAPTER 23

Crap, I'm running late. They're going to kill me. This whole thing was my idea. A way for me to rid myself of most of the money I had accumulated. I wanted to get rid of all the drug money. Money from my dad. The money I stole from my uncle. I had a little leftover but I'll make sure I do good things with it too. A way for me and everyone else that wanted the opportunity to go straight. With the family drug business closed down, people needed somewhere to work. Do real work.

I pull up to the plaza and there's already plenty of people waiting. Walking around and getting to know each other. I get out and straighten my tie in the side mirror of my truck. I used to hate wearing suits, but I can't lie, I look pretty good in them. Couldn't do the dress shoes, but nothing wrong with a nice suit and a nice pair of sneakers.

"Hey Javon," I hear Nicki call out to me.

"Hey, what's up. Shouldn't you be touring your new offices," I respond.

"Hey Von," Andrea makes her appearance known.

"Oh, hey Andrea, shouldn't you be in your shop?"

"No, this is so much more fun. Nicki and I have really been getting to know each other," both Andrea and Nicki laugh.

"Have fun," I make an awkward exit from that conversation.

I don't know if they're laughing about how Nicki curved me or how Andrea and I used to date. Either way, I don't want to be anywhere near them right now. Andrea always made little trinkets, now she has a small art shop. She'll be able to sell her trinkets and supplies. She's right next door to Nicki. She graduated just after I got shot. Now she's got a place to practice, a place where people who have the least access to therapy can meet a therapist. Nicki believes that art can be a great release for stress, and help to express the pain we feel from trauma. Putting them right next to each other was a great idea.

"Javon, come here," AC calls out to me.

"Hey, what's up. I see you already got customers," AC got his bakery and his boyfriend, or his husband now, has been killing the social media game.

"All thanks to you, finally giving us a space to make out dream come true," he gives me a big hug. I'm still not big on hugs, but you can't tell AC to get lost. He's too big.

"Nah, you been chasing the dream for a long time."

"Come by later, we'll have more of those cookies and cream cupcakes you love so much."

"You know I'll be there for those. You see Nate?"

"Yeah, he should be down at the gym."

"Thanks AC."

The gym, now that was something I didn't expect to be here. There was already a gym here. A small gym with dilapidated equipment. I was going to empty it out and rent the place out. Then Stack called me after he heard what went down. I told him what our plan was and he just had to be in on it. He was ready to grow old and just watch his kids grow up and avoiding the same mistakes he made. Even offered to put his own cash up. It was coincidence the gym was there, he wanted to open a boxing gym. Somewhere he could teach people to handle their problems without guns. I could use a couple of classes the way Grady manhandled me. Still, the first Friday of every month he runs this thing called Fight

Night. People who have beef come in and box six rounds. At the end they shake hands and squash the beef. If they don't Nicki gets involved. We all work well as a team.

Most of us are just trying to repair the damage we caused. I know I fucked up. I just didn't know other people felt guilty about the things they did. Not sure why I thought I was the only one who felt guilt. Stack and I both feel like we let my uncle ruin all codes of conduct my father set. AC felt like he should have been helping people the whole time. Nate felt like he should have never been selling drugs in the first place. This was the way we found peace. We could bring things to the neighborhood that people don't have access to. We're trying to get a grocery store here but we're kind of shooting in the dark on that one.

"I said jab, you're still throwing hooks," Stack yells out.

"Take it easy on them," I stand next to him and watch.

"If I take it easy on them, they might realize I care about them."

"Wouldn't be so bad. Both of us could have used someone to say they cared about us."

"You had people that told you they cared. You just didn't listen."

"Were you any different when you were young?"

"Yeah. I was a good kid, until I met your dad. He was a good kid. Just hard headed. Like you. Both of y'all got them big ass hard heads," he laughs at his own joke.

"You really trying to roast people with those short shorts on? Looking like a buff Magic Johnson," we both laugh. Stack isn't family by blood but he's more of an uncle than Grady ever was. Wish I saw that sooner.

"Muhammad Ali wore shorts just like this. You know, that right?"

"Yeah and he was way smaller. You about to pop out of them daisy dukes."

"You know your pops would be proud of you. You've done what he always wanted to do, but could never figure out. You got out the game, took your people with you and are giving back."

"Thanks."

"No, thank you. I thought I would die still doing that shit. But you gave me a way out nephew. Now, unless you're gonna put on some gloves, get the hell out of my gym. I know you're just dodging the people outside. You need to be spending some time with Nicki, or Andrea. I don't know how your depressing ass got two women that like you. Two? And they ain't bad looking. If I wasn't married. Boy, you don't even know. My wife would be mad at the thoughts I'm having," Stack just smiles this time.

"Alright, I'll see you later. Go take a cold shower or something."

"There you are," Nate grabs me when I walk out.

"I've been looking for you."

"Bullshit, come on. You got a speech to give."

"A speech? What do I need to give a speech for?"

"Because there are people in the community here that want to hear from you. People who know what your dad and uncle did. You need to tell them something before they burn all this down," he pushes me towards a podium in the parking lot.

"Man hold up, you're the property manager," I try to argue.

"But you're the owner."

"Where's Tevin? He can do this. He loves talking to people."

"Not here, said he was interviewing more security guards."

"Hey everyone," he's left me at the podium with no introduction or warning. "Hey, my family has kind of messed up this community."

"Kind of," an old woman asks.

"Yes, kind of. We aren't responsible for everything," probably a bad response. Several people roll their eyes.

"Look. I acknowledge we messed up. Especially my uncle. But I'm not my uncle, or my father. I'm Javon, we're going clean this place up. That's my goal. All I'm asking is that you give me a chance to help."

"And if we don't," the same old lady rolls her neck at me. I didn't know this was an interview.

"Then I'll do it anyway. You might not want my help but I'm sure somebody does."

"I say we give him a chance," Tiffany calls from the back of the crowd.

"Thank you, I won't let you down."

"You better not," the same old lady says walking away.

"Thanks for the save."

"You had a heckler," she laughs.

"Old ladies are tough. You showed me that," I laugh. I notice a teenage boy next to her when he starts to laugh.

"I'll arrest you right now Javon. I will find something. Andre, you live with me. It wasn't that funny. Javon this is my son Andre."

"Nice to meet you Andre," I shake his hand.

"Likewise," he responds. "Are you a police officer like my mom?"

I can't help but laugh. My chest hurts by the time I'm done, "me, a cop? Never."

"He's not a police officer, yet. He still needs to be worked on."

"Sure I do," I smile at her.

"Go start the car Andre," he senses something is up and heads off.

"What's up?"

"You don't need to testify. Your uncle took a plea. He's going to be doing close to sixty years before he can even apply for parole."

"That's good shit."

"Yeah, and I made lieutenant."

"I don't know what that means, but congrats."

"It means I get to lead a small team of detectives now."

"Well good job boss lady."

"You want to come with us to celebrate?"

"Are we hanging out still? I thought we would go our separate ways when this was done?"

"I don't have a lot of family. Your dad was like family, so you're family."

"Alright, let's go before I have to give another speech."

"You've still got the biggest speech to give," Nate jumps in.

"What speech is that?"

"At the court," Stack adds his input.

"Why would I be giving a speech at the court?"

"You have to testify," Nicki pops in.

"Yeah, testify goofy," Andrea laughs at me.

"But I thought he took a plea deal?"

"Nah man, you have to set the record straight," AC hands me a cookie.

"Oh, my brother, testify," Tevin jokes.

☐

CHAPTER 24

"Javon get up," Nate starts shaking me.

"What? Leave me alone. I was having a good dream. Just let me sleep," I try to shove him away.

"Man c'mon. The car ride wasn't long enough for you to be falling asleep."

"I'm just tired."

"No, you're taking those damn pills again. I told you to quit taking those," Nate is unreasonably mad.

"You're not my mom," I try to make a joke.

"You wouldn't listen to her anyway. C'mon man. You look a fucking mess. You're about to have one of the biggest moments of your life and you're over here drooling on yourself. You look like Ned the Wino. C'mon, get it together. Why are you still taking those pills?"

"I got shot man. It hurts."

"It probably did hurt when you got shot, and after the surgery to fix your shoulder, but that was months ago. You don't need those pills anymore. You're the last person I wanted to see fucked up like this. You were always talking about being the leader, now look at you," I can tell I've let Nate down.

It hurts more than I thought it would. He leads me through the metal detectors and into the courthouse. I always liked this building; it gives me the feeling that I'm tiny. Almost as if, in the grand scheme of things my life is meaningless. I'm not as important as I thought I was. Maybe other people matter just as much. I think that might be the pills talking, or the guilt, been pretty hard to tell the difference lately. I've got a lot of people depending on me today. Tiffany went against the rules, if we don't get a conviction, she might get fired instead of promoted. Nate is a marked man, since everyone knows we're friends. He even moved out the neighborhood and started staying with me because he was scared and didn't want his parent's house shot up. Tevin is in the wind, maybe dead. I hope not. This is the chance to get justice for my dad, and all the people my uncle killed. Victims of the drugs we sold and everyone else. Nate leads me to the bathroom where he tries to fix me up for court.

I get a good look at myself in the mirror, and I've really fallen off. I've got a nice lineup but my hair is kinky and rolled up, I've started to grow a beard that fans out in patches all going different directions. I do have drool on my face, sleep in my eyes, my entire suit is crooked and twisted. I ask Nate to grab me some water and snacks from the vending machine, while I stare at myself in the mirror a little longer. I don't know what I expect to happen. Some mirror person to come out and shake me or switch places.

I'm probably going to regret this. I lean over the toilet and stick my finger down my throat. Soon I'm vomiting up the pills I had a few minutes ago. My throat burns and my mouth is filled with the taste of vomit. I'm not done yet; I pour all the pills I have left into the toilet and flush. Something just told me, I don't need them. I mean, Nate's been telling me that, but this felt more powerful. Something about this building as if this was the moment my life would change. I use the paper towels to wash and dry my face so I look presentable before fixing my suit. I just can't seem to fix this tie. Fuck it, I never was a tie person anyway. I toss the tie into the trash as Nate walks back into the bathroom. I force myself to eat the granola bar and down a bottle of water as fast as possible. I'm not sure if it helps alleviate the high, I've already got, maybe I'm thinking hangover. At least it gets the taste of vomit out of my mouth.

"Nate, I've never said this before, but I'm sorry," I extend my hand.

"You've said it a lot. Just get your shit together," he walks out the bathroom without shaking my hand.

Can't say I didn't deserve that. I just follow his lead for now. I don't even know which court room we're going to and he's been more coherent than I have during this whole process. After a couple of turns we meet Tiffany at the elevator. She greets Nate and I while pretending she isn't worried. She goes over everything with me. What kind of questions the defense team will ask, what kind of answers I should give. Apparently, they had practice classes for all the people testifying, but I was too high to show up. Inside the elevator she presses the stop button. Almost immediately the palm of her hand crosses my face, I can't help but feel like I'd rather be shot again.

"Why the fuck would you show up to court high," she slaps Nate before I can answer. "You need to be a better friend and watch him," Nate backs away after his slap, afraid of Tiffany.

"But I'm not his parent," he mumbles under his breath with his head down.

"Hey, Nate is a great friend. Better than I deserve. He told me I shouldn't be taking those pills. I just didn't listen. But it's over now. I flushed them all," I focus on not slurring any of my words or falling asleep mid-sentence.

"Nate, I'm sorry. I shouldn't have slapped you," Tiffany apologizes to Nate. Then she slaps me again.

"Okay, enough with the slaps. I'm good," I'm grateful for the shabby beard and the little protection it gives me. She hits hard. I'm feeling like Jay-Z over here.

"No, you're not good until you're done on the stand," she presses the button to signal the elevator to move again.

I know when it's better to shut up than to keep talking. I don't even try to plead my case. I just do as I'm told and follow along. I take a seat in the back of the court room with the other witnesses while Nate and Tiffany sit up front.

I just wait until my name is called. It isn't long, I'm the first witness of the day. I'm quickly sworn in on the Bible, they don't offer me anything else. How do they even know if I'm religious? Doesn't matter at this point. I take my seat on the stand and try to look as sober as possible.

"Mr. Swift," the lawyer starts his questioning. "How do you know the defendant, and how long?"

"He's my uncle. Known him all my life."

"Would you say he's a kind man?"

"He shot me after he confessed to killing my father, so no I wouldn't call him kind."

"Do you believe your uncle participated in the narcotics trade."

"I know he did."

"How do you know that?"

"I saw it."

"How?"

"I worked for him," there's a few audible gasps in the court room. Tiffany facepalms and Nate put his head down. I suppose I should have plead the fifth there.

"So, you want us to believe the word of a drug dealer? That's not a very strong word to go on," the lawyer starts.

"Yeah, I do, because I'm telling the truth. Who walks up to the stand and confesses to a crime for no reason? I'm just being honest here. I fucked up; I admit it. I want to be better and part of that is helping put his ass behind bars."

"Enough with the swearing," the judge interrupts.

"I'm sorry ma'am," I apologize and she looks shocked. "I'm sorry your honor," she nods in acceptance.

"Mr. Swift, you are an adult. How can you blame someone else for your actions," the lawyer continues his questioning?

"I blame myself. I should have found another way than letting him manipulate me. My dad died, I didn't know any other way, he made me drop out of college and threatened to leave me homeless. I could give excuses all day as to why and how he took advantage of me. I'm guilty, but not like him, and that's the reason he's on trial right now," I cross my arms feeling satisfied with my answer.

The rest of the questions go by in a blur. I should have plead the fifth a few times. I didn't want to seem guilty. I mean, I am guilty, I just didn't want to give them any reason to doubt me. I feel like most of the questions were just to get under my skin. Questions about my sexual orientation, did I feel neglected by mother, was this revenge against her and if my father was a drug addict. They asked me almost nothing about the case. I got flustered, it probably would have been worse if I was high out of my mind.

Nate and Tiffany stayed inside to hear the verdict. I wanted to go outside, get some air, cool off and maybe stretch my legs. I've been laying around doing nothing but popping pills and playing video games since the middle of December now it feels like I have to do something. After being drilled about how bad I was all while trying to be the friendly neighborhood drug dealer, maybe I need to find a positive way to help. I make my way across the street to the city market and sit in the small courtyard. Maybe I'll be a farmer.

I spend what seems like hours staring into the sky like some kind of weirdo. I'm glad it's cloudy outside today, otherwise I'd be staring right into the sun. Tiffany and Nate make their way over to me with big smiles on their faces. I guess that means my uncle was found guilty. Good enough for me.

"You sucked on stand," Tiffany says "but you were the deciding factor in the jury's ruling."

"So, how'd it go," I ask as if I couldn't tell.

"He's guilty, we have to wait until sentencing but the prosecution recommended 20 years to life, he'll get at least 15," Nate fills me in.

"That's great. Can we go get something to eat," I ask. Knowing he's going to jail is all I need.

"What did you have in mind? My treat," Tiffany offers.

"How about we stop at AC's bakery. I want some sweets," dude can really bake.

"AC doesn't have a bakery," Nate interjects.

"Who is AC," Tiffany asks.

"Oh, I must have been dreaming. Let's head to the cop spot then. I'll tell you both all about it. You were there."

ABOUT THE AUTHOR

Darrell Shaffer has been alive for a quarter of a century and accomplished very little. He's had dinner with two mayors, a governor and too many CEO's to count. He however has not done any of those things. Instead he carves out a living working day to day like the rest of us.

He spends his nights writing, hoping someone will enjoy his work. He spends his weekends hoping the next YouTube video he makes will go viral. In the meantime, he will continue working until age 67 so that he can retire and conquer a neighboring galaxy.

You can read more of Darrell's work at
www.12AMFiction.com